Feather
for
Hoonah Joe

Alaska Can Be a Very Small Place

Marianne Schlegelmilch

One of America's Most Gifted Writers

Since 1978

PO Box 221974 Anchorage, Alaska 99522-1974
books@publicationconsultants.com—www.publicationconsultants.com

ISBN 978-1-59433-464-1
eISBN 978-1-59433-465-8
Library of Congress Catalog Card Number: 2014936037

Cover Art by Barb Montpas Sirmeyer

Manufactured in the United States of America.

A Note about the Cover Artist

When I began *Feather for Hoonah Joe,* I wanted to concentrate on two of my favorite characters, Sal and Joe. When suddenly a storyline emerged, I found it exciting to see how I could further develop the characters of these two elders.

The story, *Feather for Hoonah Joe,* has been a personal journey for me because along the way, not only did I recover my inspiration to continue writing, but the cover artist is someone I first knew in third grade.

This special collaboration was made more meaningful by the fact that we ourselves are now elders like two of the main characters I wrote about, and by the fact that we worked from about 4,000 miles apart to make this happen.

My personal thanks to Barb Montpas Sirmeyer for the special and beautiful cover art for *Feather for Hoonah Joe,* and also for all she has done to encourage me.

Marianne Schlegelmilch

Dedication

In Memory of Arne Bulkeley Beltz of Rhinebeck and Alaska
(1917-2013)

Table of Contents

Chapter One
Where's Sal?

Doug Williams threw the last piece of luggage into the back of the Suburban just as the rapid-fire sound of three gunshots, followed ten seconds later by a single shot, sent him ducking for cover behind his vehicle.

Frozen in place by the gunfire, he stopped himself from calling out to Mara, while saying a silent prayer that she was okay. Maybe this was only someone messing around with seals or doing some of the other stupid things that people seemed to do every spring after a long, dark Alaska winter had kept them cooped up for too long.

He hunkered down, waiting to see if the gunshots resumed. Instinctively he reached inside his vest pocket for his pistol, racked a bullet into the chamber, and then said another prayer that she was okay.

He heard her call before he saw her.

"Mara!" he yelled, stepping out from behind the Suburban, his hand still on his pistol, as he watched her run toward him from the opposite end of the boardwalk that held their cabin. He pointed the gun at the ground, afraid to put it away just yet. Behind Mara hurried their equally frantic, elderly, and most special friend, Joe Michael.

Doug had seldom seen his wife as beside herself as she was right now. Something was wrong.

Mara huddled beside him, and then quickly inched over to make room for Joe Michael. The old man raised himself up onto his toes to meet Doug chest to chest, as if to ensure that their eye contact would be as clear and forthright as his words. He balanced himself with one hand on the deck rail, while he used the other one to push his eyeglasses up onto the bridge of his nose. Then he took a long, deep breath followed by two shorter ones, steadied himself, and spoke.

"We gotta find her, Doug. We only got a coupla more hours before dark."

"What's this about, Joe?"

"Sal's missing," Mara said.

"That's why I fired off the shots," Joe added, lowering himself to his normal standing position before finding a nearby bench to sit down on. "That's our distress signal—three quick shots and then a fourth. She didn't fire back. That's our other signal—if one of us fires and the other doesn't fire back, then something's wrong."

Doug put his pistol back into the shoulder holster he wore 90 percent of the time. Its comfortable weight rested against his chest.

Joe Michael put his head down into his hands looking deflated, diminutive, and frail. A lifetime of tragedy had taken its toll on the seventy-four year-old man. After spending much of his life looking out for others, he now needed to ask others to help him—not that he ever had to ask Doug and Mara for anything. There was no question that they were there for him and it had been that way ever since Joe had given Mara the feather that had changed her life. But it went against his nature to lean on others, and that included the young couple that he considered as dear as a son and a daughter.

"Settle down, okay? We all know that Sal takes off all the time," Doug said.

He paced back and forth and then did it again. Could either of them sense how much he was struggling to remain calm, how desperately he was trying to find the right words—the right actions—to make everything okay? He listened as Mara spilled out the details of what had just happened.

Just minutes earlier, she had come home from shopping to find Joe frantic and pacing outside their cabin door. He had told her that Sal was missing. She had helped him search for her, walking around both cabins, and then searched inside them only to find no sign of Sal—not even a note or message of any kind.

"I'm really worried, Doug," she said. "I've never known Joe to be this upset."

Doug stared at the tired-looking old man. The old Joe would already have been in his skiff out looking for his wife.

He tightened his jaw, increasing his grip on Joe and Mara's shoulders at the same time. He had almost lost them before, too many times to count, and he would not—could not—risk losing either of them again.

"Couldn't Sal have just gone out to run some errands? Maybe she went for a walk," he said.

"Then why didn't she respond to my signal?" Joe said, looking up at them both.

"But I just saw you two working on your cabin this morning, Joe. It got me to thinking that you two were just about done getting Stu's cabin fixed up just the way you want it. Sal seemed fine then."

"She was, okay?" Joe answered. "But lately—look, having you and Mara next door is the only reason we even come to Juneau and bother with my brother's old place. Sal hasn't been herself for about a year now. I don't know if she's unhappy or just losin' track of where she lives . . . I don't know. Maybe I should just think about selling the cabin and keeping her at home in Hoonah. Maybe it's all too much for people our age."

"Wait, now—you think Sal's run off because she's unhappy, or worse yet, because she's losing her faculties?" Doug asked. "Well, at least you don't think its foul play of some kind. Right?"

Joe shook his head.

Doug paced the dock for several minutes while Mara sat next to Joe on one of the benches that lined the boardwalk. Joe was not one to make flippant comments. What *was* going on? Had he and Mara missed the signs of mental decline that Joe was alluding to? Was Sal not only missing, but also no longer competent enough to find her way out of whatever mess she had gotten herself into?

"Let's get Thor and see if he can track Sal down," Doug said. "Thor! C'mere! We gotta go!"

"Thor's gone, too," Mara answered, "and so is my skiff."

Thor would have done everything to keep Sal from harm, and would have come for him if something bad had happened to Sal. That meant that none of this could be an accident, unless Thor was injured or something.

"Did Sal say anything this morning that might help us figure out where she went?" Doug asked.

"She said something about needing to keep an eye on the shoreline," Joe said. "She's been saying that a lot since they had that TV special about the tsunami debris from Japan moving this way. She seems kind of fixated on it if you want the truth. I don't know why. I told her there's nothin' we can do about it anyway."

Doug put one arm around the old man's shoulders and guided him back to his cabin, while Mara went ahead to check once more for any sign of Sal—scurrying from their cabin to Joe and Sal's, and then back again to their own.

He understood Mara's distress. Sal had been like a mother to her in the same way that Joe had been like a father. The two elders had married only a few years before and, well, that was another story . . .

Now that he thought about it, though, there had been small signs that something was amiss with Sal. Just a few weeks ago, he and Mara had taken the *Driftfeather* over to Hoonah to visit Joe and Sal and had noticed that she had seemed distracted—maybe even forgetful. He hadn't thought much about it at the time, but now, in view of what Joe was saying—well, maybe there *was* something odd going on with her.

Then there was the time a few months ago when Sal had come aboard the seiner like she always did, but had referred to it as her own, and referred to Joe as Bert—the name of her deceased first husband with whom she had once owned the *Driftfeather*. Quickly realizing her mistake, she had laughed the whole thing off, while hugging Joe and reminding him that he was her sweet baby now.

Doug laughed wryly and out loud. He knew that no one but Sal would get away with calling Joe Michael *sweet baby*. The thought made the fact that Sal was missing seem as though a ship had been lost at sea. Sal was bigger than life, and her presence in his world and Mara's was the reason they were together right now—at least that's what he chose to believe.

He watched Mara check both cabins for the second time. She, too, had mentioned a couple of strange incidents with Sal, but Sal was eighty now, and it had been easy enough to chalk the missteps up to the fact that maybe all of them were getting a little forgetful now and then.

Sal had always been self-reliant, and it was not unusual for her to disappear and return when she was good and ready, but this time something about her disappearance was alarming her normally stoic husband, and that was its own concern.

"Since the day we married, Sal's never left my side without leaving me a note in that hen scratch she calls writing," Joe said, forcing out a weak chuckle. "Half the time I couldn't even read it, but there was always a note."

Sal might be feisty, but Doug had never known her to do anything to worry the man she called *her Joey*. And she often took Thor along with her, so that alone was not a concern except for the fact that she usually told someone she was taking him. No, something was wrong and now he was as concerned as Joe and Mara were. He would immediately launch the rescue for the 5-foot-1-inch old lady with the 6-foot-4-inch persona who they all knew as Sal Kindle. When Mara came out of Joe's cabin he announced his plan of action.

"I'm gonna get the skiff off the *Driftfeather* and we'll take a look around the shoreline. Pack up a couple of extra blankets, too, Mara. Snow's forecast for tonight and they say that isn't any April fool, even though it would make a good one if only Sal weren't out there having to face April under who-knows-what condition she's in. And Joe, you stick with me. We'll find her. I promise you that."

Joe raised his head and flashed Doug a hopeful look before again staring at the ground as he shuffled along behind him.

Chapter Two
Home for Now

A heavy fog had settled over Auke Bay. The rumbling sound of an approaching raft moved toward them as Doug and the others putted along one with the haze, several miles from the harbor.

"That's her," Joe said, pointing to what was clearly the silhouette of a woman and a dog in the dinghy.

Minutes later Doug had maneuvered their skiff close enough to see that it was indeed Sal sitting on the back seat of the raft, guiding the motor with one arm. Standing with his front paws on the forward seat as if navigating them both across the bay, was his ocean-loving wolf-dog, Thor.

"Hell's afire, is that you Jane? And you brought Doug and my Joe along with ya? Don't ya know only a fool goes out on the water at night this time of year in Alaska?"

"Thank God you're okay, Sal," Joe said, slightly raising the tone of his normally soft, rhythmic voice. "We've been looking everywhere. Wasn't no note, no sign of you. You always tell me where you're going . . ."

For once Sal had nothing to say.

"We'll follow you in," Doug said, letting Sal take the lead as they moved through the heavy fog like mere shadows across the bay. The gentle slapping of their rafts against the water made the only sound—that and the dull hum of their motors.

"I'm fine, ya know," Sal suddenly spurted, before pulling up to the dock to let Thor jump out and then guiding the raft under Mara's cabin, where she tied it up.

Doug pulled up behind her, waiting until she moved off to let Joe and Mara climb onto the dock behind Thor. Then he moved ahead, letting his raft idle in the water behind Sal.

"I'll pull up and give you a hand if you need it, Sal."

"I got it," she snapped.

He watched the old woman climb out of the skiff and deftly tie it up as she had obviously done hundreds of times in her life. Even at eighty she was able to climb up the ladder to the deck, and she did so now without as much as a glance back his way. Knowing her to have always been fiercely independent, he knew to back off when Sal told him to. Today she seemed especially annoyed.

When he got up to their cabin, Mara was making coffee and Sal and Joe were sitting at the kitchen table talking quietly, with Joe's hand resting on Sal's arm.

"You take two sugars, right Sal?" Mara asked.

"Yup. But maybe ya better make it three taday since I seem to be causin' everyone ta worry about me takin' off without tellin' ya, like I ain't smart enough ta manage ta make a decision after bein' on this earth for longer 'n the two a ya been alive even if ya totaled yer ages."

Mara brought the coffee to the table, setting the mugs down in each of their four places.

"I'll just let you handle your own sugar," she told Sal, gently rubbing the old woman's shoulder.

"I think I'll plan on us heading back to Hoonah tomorrow. That be all right, honey?" Joe said softly to Sal.

"Whatever ya think, Joey," Sal murmured contritely.

Chapter Three
Girl Talk

The next day Doug helped Joe carry the rest of his and Sal's luggage to the SUV, urging him to be careful not to slip on the frost-covered wooden deck, while Mara sat with Sal in the cabin. The old man was unusually quiet, not responding to a couple of Doug's bland comments about the weather, so Doug just helped him load several bags and then busied himself, while Joe shuffled his way back to his cabin.

"I want ya ta stop worryin' about me, Jane. Everyone's actin' like I'm daft or somethin'," Sal said to Mara as the two sipped coffee.

"Well, it's just that we all love you, Sal, and—"

"Look, Jane, there ain't no need ta worry. I ain't crazy and I ain't feeble and I ain't losin' my faculties or anything like that, okay?"

Mara gave Sal a gentle hug.

"Jest because I forgot a coupla things fer a minute here an' there don't mean I'm some old geezer that needs a bunch a protection from myself, ya know. Haven't ya ever slipped up? Huh?"

"Okay, Sal. I'm sorry if we overreacted. Joe loves you so much and Doug and I do, too."

"Well, ya don't need ta kill me with kindness or smother me with the warm fuzzies, Jane. Hell's a blazin', how'd ya think I made it this far in life? Do ya think someone babysat me fer the last eighty years? Well, think about that, Jane. I ain't no helpless old broad wearin' granny diapers, ya know."

"I'm sorry, Sal, but barking at me is not going to make me worry one iota less about you and the sooner you figure that out, the better we're going to get along here."

Mara stifled the urge to smile. Everyone knew you didn't talk back to Sal and certainly you didn't laugh about it if you did.

Sal kept her tongue as she got up and carried her empty mug back inside and placed it in the sink. Why were they all so danged worried about her anyway? Did they think she should be sitting in a rocking chair and only getting up to stir the soup and change her apron? Because if that's what they thought—

"Don't worry about the dishes, Sal. I'll take care of them later."

"Ya know, there's gonna be a lotta stuff floatin' on over here from that big tsunami they had over there in Japan. That means there's gonna be money ta be made, Jane. I'm jest tryin' ta figure out how I can work it for me 'n Joe and you and yer old man."

"You know his name is Doug, Sal. And the debris is not necessarily coming here."

So this was what was on Sal's mind.

"Besides, they say it's radioactive. They're also saying we need to respect the property of the Japanese people and—"

"Blah, blah, blah, Jane. Respect is as respect does and yakkety yak yak. I'm tellin' ya there's money out there. Now, I ain't sayin' I'm gonna snatch some poor widow's diamond ring offa dead skeleton floatin' on by—"

"Sal!"

"It's jest a figure a speech, Jane. Don't get all righteous on me, okay? What ya don't know is that Bert and me made enough money on salvage ta buy both the *Storm Roamer* and the *Driftfeather*. Seiners like them don't come cheap as ya already learned. Now if things pan out like I think they're gonna, then the four of us stand to make a tidy sum outta the remains a that tidal wave and no one's gonna get disrespected or hurt exceptin' the four of us if we don't jump on this opportunity before anyone else gets the same idea."

"Well, I know the Coast Guard just sank that ship off of Sitka the other day," Mara answered, "but I hadn't really given it much more thought."

"Look, the Feds is already messin' with fishin' quotas and things are a blastin' mess with knowin' how anyone's gonna make a dime offa fishin' anymore, so we need ta be smart and start plannin' ahead, that's all I'm sayin'."

Sal grabbed a sponge and began to wipe the table.

"Yer jest as bad as my Joey, Jane. Ain't no entrepreneurial spirit in neither of ya."

Chapter Four

Beachmoppers, Inc.

For the next month Mara spent most of her spare time getting KonaJane's ready for the first cruise ship of the season. It arrived in Juneau by mid-May, just as the work was finished. Doug had helped her by painting the outside of the shop, resealing all the roof vents, and repairing some of the loose planks in the deck, while she had scrubbed the walls and floors inside and completely deep cleaned the kitchen area. Together they had hauled the outdoor tables out of storage and inserted huge yellow and blue umbrellas into holes in the centers—a look that brought the dark green building to life.

On the last day of May, Doug had set out on his first fishing trip of the season—he captaining the *Storm Roamer,* and his longtime friend and crew-member, Derrk Stanley, the *Driftfeather.* They had decided over the winter that Mara would work hard to get KonaJane's profitable that summer, while Doug would become familiar with the fisheries in their area that would allow him to make a living while still returning home at least weekly.

"When ya comin' west, Jane?" Sal bellowed into Mara's smartphone one afternoon in early June. "Me'n my Joe's been out almost every day checkin' things out and I'm tellin' ya, it's worse than they said."

Mara listened as Sal told her about the massive amounts of debris washing up on the beaches of outer islands all along the Gulf of Alaska.

"Ya know that place where we all beached our seiners that day right before ya married yer ole man?"

"Can't you call him Doug?"

"Yeah, Doug, okay? Anyway, it's chock-full a nothin' but driftwood covered with old insulation, pieces a broken cabinets, torn clothing, shoes . . . Ya name it, Jane, and it's out there. Soon as my Joey saw the mess, he was all in on the deal. Finally saw the potential, jest like I said."

"Have you been cataloging it? Selling it? Returning it? Exactly what are you doing with what you find?" Mara asked, feigning interest in the endeavor while she made a couple of cappuccinos for some customers who had come in moments before.

"Well, the first thing I figured out was that haulin' it all away was gonna be a big problem," Sal said. "I mean, haul it ta where?

The second thing I learned was that there's so much of it, that mosta the usual buyers are already contractin' out to regular debris collectors."

"Already? One moment, Sal . . ."

"That'll be $5.50," she told her customers after placing the phone on the counter. "Okay, I'm back now. You were saying."

"So, Joe and me, well, we had ta make a decision on jest what we was gonna do ta stay—what can I say, Jane—marketable, ya know. The answer's gonna shock ya, so I hope yer sittin' down."

"I'm not but I will, Sal—not that I can think of anything that you do that would shock me."

Mara smiled. It was wonderful to hear Sal sounding like her old self again with none of the forgetfulness that she had shown a few months ago now evident.

"Very funny, Jane," Sal said, bringing her back to the present. "Now ya gonna keep interuptin'me with drivel or ya gonna listen up?"

"Lay it on me, Sal," Mara laughed. "But hurry, because I see a couple of people wandering over this way."

"Joe and me, well, we figured there wasn't no money in collectin' the debris ourselves—'specially when ya consider all the fuel costs and even the time we had to spend comin' and goin'. Besides, we ain't as young as we were when Bert and me was salvagin'. So, anyway," Sal said, stopping to catch her breath, "we started up our own debris recovery business called Beachmoppers, Inc. Hired us a coupla college students, bought an old landing craft that was about to be scrapped, and set about pickin' up contracts, while sendin' our staff out to pick up debris."

"So, how's the business doing so far, Sal?"

"Well, let's jest say we got us two crews and are in the process a buyin' an old storage building in the boatyard to turn inta a sortin' facilty," Sal said." Seems like these collectors is gettin' pretty persnickety about how they want their stuff brought in. Yup. T'ain't like the old days when me 'n Bert used ta haul everythin' . . ."

Sal's voice suddenly became muffled as she began talking to someone else.

"Love ya, too, sweet baby," she called, before returning to her conversation with Mara. "That was my Joey."

"I figured," Mara answered. "Maybe Doug and I will take one of our seiners over to Hoonah next week. We miss you both, you know."

"Yeah, back at ya, Jane. Anyways, Joey and I should be the proud owners a the old storage shed at the boatyard in Hoonah by jest about this time tomorrow."

"How big is it, Sal?"

"Big enough for all the junk and with enough room to dry dock two seiners, too, if we need to do any work, ya know. It's gonna need a coat a paint. Well, maybe I can hire us a coupla—"

"Doug and I can help paint," Mara interrupted.

"Couldn't ask that, Jane. Ya two's got yer own thing goin' . . ."

"How about if we just call it our vacation and show up for the week before solstice?" Mara insisted.

Konajane's would be fine with the help of the regulars she hired each summer during their college breaks. She would concentrate on building the business next year.

"Well, okay, Jane. Okay," Sal answered, not even pretending to try to dissuade her.

"Gotta go, Sal. More customers. See you soon."

Chapter Five
Solstice

Despite their plans to dedicate the full summer to their own endeavors, Doug was up for the idea of spending summer solstice in Hoonah and for painting Sal's new building—what Mara laughingly called his sense of adventure and spontaneity. By the second week of June he had already obtained enough paint and equipment to haul over on the *Driftfeather*.

Meanwhile, Derrk had agreed to hire a crew to help him and his son take the *Storm Roamer* out for the entire month. At Doug's insistence, Derrk had agreed to take a percentage of the profits in addition to a generous salary in return for his help in keeping his fishing enterprise going for the summer.

"It's only fair," he had told his loyal friend.

A week later, with only two days left before solstice, Doug, Mara, Joe, and Sal put the final red trim on the old boat shed they had painted gray. When the group of college students they had hired to paint the company name on the side of the shed suggested a mural instead, the four jumped at the idea, cheering the team on as they worked.

Although the business would be known as Beachmoppers on paper, around Hoonah it readily became known as The Gallery—the place with the colorful scenes depicting beaches full of empty boxes and tsunami debris painted on the side, with the lower right hand corner of the mural illustrating Sal and Joe in their recovery vessel dragging a net full of debris up the ramp with a loader.

Sal and Mara held an open house on the day of the summer solstice that included performances by two local bands as well as an array of community artists who were set up under canopies outside of Beachmoppers. Inside, they held a sale featuring, among other treasures, a large array of rubber floats that

Sal's crews had salvaged from the beaches. They also provided twice-daily personal tours of the new facility.

As luck would have it, a small cruise ship had docked for the day, bringing in an eclectic array of tourists who seemed to be mostly from New York, and whose enthusiasm for all things labeled as Japanese tsunami debris sent Sal scurrying to their beached landing craft by midafternoon to look for a few more things to sell.

When she got to the scrapyard that Joe had leased from the state, she went aboard the vessel, just to make sure everything was secure. Then she returned to her truck and drove to their adjacent lot to look for more floats.

Initially, they had stored everything they salvaged on that lot. Now that most everything had been moved to the new facility, just a couple of trucks and trailers, and a few odds and ends that still needed to be moved remained. She made a mental note to hire someone to mow down the weeds before next week when the landing craft was due in from its next excursion and the lot would be filled again.

From her pickup, she spotted an elderly woman with a slight build whose choice of lightweight designer summer wear immediately labeled her as a tourist.

"Probably one of the boat people from New York," she snickered under her breath. "I'm sorry, ma'am, but the sale's back at the big shed at the boatyard," she said out loud.

The elderly woman continued approaching, undeterred by Sal's remarks.

"Well, if I could have ever guessed where you'd been hiding all these years, it never would have been on this remote island in Alaska, Sylvia," the woman said, displaying no sign of surprise at encountering the older sister she hadn't seen since she was a sixteen-year-old student at boarding school and Sal was a twenty-one year old college graduate.

Sal stepped back. Could that really be who she thought it was? She looked downward, pretending to busy herself, while she collected her thoughts. Was there nowhere on earth that a body could escape to? Even after sixty years, the pain of their separation remained as fresh as if it were yesterday, only now the hurt had been replaced with anger at having been forced out of the comfortable life from which she had been forced to flee.

"Hidin' I ain't, and welcomin' the likes a you I ain't either, Elzianne. What ya want here anyway? Gettin' bored with yer society friends?" Sal answered, addressing her estranged younger sister and ready with one of the quick retorts that had always marked any of their conversations—the long years having done little to dim either their recognition of, or contempt for each other.

"Oh dear, Sylvia. Did you develop that charming folksy accent while you were at Yale, or did it just come to you from living life on the run up here in the closest place to Siberia where you could still keep your citizenship—and abide by the terms of the trust mother set up for you?"

Sal flinched at the reference to her obviously altered speech pattern, one that she had carefully developed in her mission to divest herself of all remnants of her past.

"What would you know about me, my citizenship, or anything else, Elzi? Get outta my life once and fer all. I spent half my adult life tryin' ta make ya love me—sendin' ya letters, plane tickets, leavin' ya messages ya never returned—but ya could never put aside yer life's mission ta envy my every move to even see any goodness in me, so ya been dead to me ever since I finally saw ya fer what ya was, and dead to me yer gonna stay."

"Now, Sylvia, as touched as I am by your kind reminder of our sisterly love, I'd like to interrupt the accolades to snap a photo of you to share with the rest of the family—and especially with Bert's surviving nephew, who is firmly convinced, by the way, that his uncle's loss at sea was no accident . . ."

"Git offa this island, ya connivin' wannabe," Sal hollered. "Ya don't know beans about me or my Bert and if yer in contact with his slimy lawyer nephew, it can only mean yer still tryin' ta come between me and my Bert just like ya always did—and don't think he didn't show me all the love letters you sent under the guise of checking on me over the years. The only difference now is ya only got his memory left ta mess with, cause ya ain't getting' ta me anymore no matter how hard ya try."

"Why, Sylvia, how can you blame me like this when all I ever wanted was to be like you."

"Be like me or be me, Elzi? Ya always been too lazy ta even carve out yer own identity in life, and it's more'n plain that ya been listenin' ta—or more'n likely creatin'—all the lies and rumors that's been floatin' through the ranks since Bert and I left the confines of Rhinebeck and all the love the parade a nannies hired by our mother could buy."

"Well, mother was good enough to look out for both of our futures. And call me naïve, Sylvia, but why would she lie about something as serious as insider trading and the pending criminal indictment about to be handed down to the then CEO of our local investment firm, your own Bert Kindle."

"Bert Kindle was a good and honest man, Elzianne Jeanette LaMonte—you did take your maiden name after your Hollywood leading man left you for his younger male co-star didn't you?" Sal shot back, speaking for the first time in the succinct and perfect English that reflected her education and upbringing.

"How did you know about—?"

"It was right there on the front page of every scandal sheet in every super-market in America—but then, you have people who shop for you, don't you, Elzi, so you can claim you didn't see them?"

Sal left no time for Elzi to respond before continuing.

"On the other hand, maybe our dear mother was the one who was, shall we say, scurrilously involved with not just the insider trading, but the man who orchestrated it, Bert's own father, Jameson Kindle, who was too busy wooing her with his charms to stop his goons from trying to frame his own son."

"Ooh, Sylvia, I didn't mean to upset you," Elzi said, recovering her aplomb and answering with the expressionless smile and coolness born of years of speaking down to most everyone in her life. "At our age—well, we must remain civil lest we risk affecting our health and all . . . you know. Surely you realize that Jameson fired everyone of those who tried to drag Bert down, but by then, you and Bert had already left."

"I would like to invite you to leave—go back to whatever it is you do now," Sal said, again speaking with perfect diction and with a restraint that surprised even her.

Turning her back on Elzianne, she threw a couple of floats into the bed of her pickup before climbing inside just as her husband drove up.

"Sal. What's going on? Everyone's looking for you back at the Gallery." Joe Michael said, stepping down from the running board of his one-ton dualie.

"Jest talkin' ta one a the touri, Joey," Sal answered. "I'm gonna follow ya back right now, matter a fact."

"Does the lady need a lift?" Joe asked.

"She says she'll be fine enough, sweet baby," Sal called to Joe before leaning out her pickup window and hissing to Elzi, "If I so much as see a thread from your Chanel suit on this island ever again, Elzianne, you are going to rue the day you tried to bring your kind of disgusting innuendo anywhere near the people and the place that I love."

From his side mirror, Joe Michael watched the exchange, none the wiser when the smile on Sal's face perfectly disguised her full-blown contempt for the sister who had spent an entire lifetime trying to bring her down.

"I'm afraid you won't be able to avoid me, dear sister," Elzi said, handing Sal her card that read:

Elzianne Jeanette LaMonte
Curator/Buyer
New York Cultural Museum

"I'm here on official business and I do so look forward to again seeing you and the charming little man who seems so smitten with you these days."

Sal was halfway up the road before she even tried to slow her old beater truck down, leaving Elzianne LaMonte a mere dust-covered dot in her rear-view mirror and leaving Joe to wonder what had gotten into her when she slammed on the brakes and just missed sliding into the ditch in order to avoid rear-ending him at the far end of a blind curve right before the boatyard.

"My boot got caught between the gas pedal and the console, Joey," was all Sal said, as Joe helped her unload the floats and carry them inside.

Chapter Six
Palmer

By the time the cruise ship left that afternoon, Sal had already locked up the shed and headed back home, pleading a headache. Meanwhile, Joe, Doug, and Mara went into town to enjoy the solstice festivities there, even though Joe's long face made it hard for any of them to really enjoy all the food and gaiety that always marked the longest day of the year in Alaska.

When Doug and Mara left to go back to Juneau, Sal seemed to be her old self again as the two couples made plans to meet in Palmer for the delayed wedding reception their friends had promised them after their remarriage the previous year.

~ ~ ~

"Let's promise to never let this happen again," Ellie said, hugging them both as if she would never let them go the minute they arrived at her homestead near Palmer.

"Glad to have you back, son," Ellie's husband, Ben, told Doug.

"There's not a day I haven't thought of you," Ben told his former daughter-in-law, as they sat around the array of tables set up in the yard of the homestead where both Doug and Mara had spent so much of her time in Alaska.

"Sarah, can you ever forgive me," Mara told her best friend, gasping as she saw how big Ken's and her baby, B.D., had become. "He's almost two, right?"

"Terrible two," Sarah laughed as B.D. tried to wriggle out of her arms.

The homestead looked the same—comfortable and familiar, with memories of the happy times there somehow overshadowing the far more frequent moments of horror that had sent all of their lives on one unbelievable detour after another. Yet still, for Mara and for Doug, this was their real Alaska home—this place up Knik River Road near the river that trickled down the mountainside from the massive Knik Glacier above.

Along with the others, they spent most of the day outdoors, enjoying a rare sunny day in the otherwise cool and rainy summer. Ellie's daughter Anna, now a preteen, was clearly enjoying some quality time with Thor in between her duties helping her mother play hostess to the barbecue that brought folks from all over Palmer to welcome Doug and Mara "home."

"You bought *two* seiners!" Ben teased them. "Next thing you know you'll have a fleet."

"We'd love to take you out with us whenever you want," Doug offered, handing Ben their address and phone number. "All you gotta do is show up."

"Won't be this year," Ben smiled, looking at Ellie. "Our baby's due in five months."

Mara smiled, thinking of how the two had found love after so much tragedy had marked their lives.

"Why, you're hardly even showing yet?" she teased her friend.

"Pretty surprising since I just learned this morning that it's twins," Ellie said, turning to see the look of surprise on her husband's face.

"Twins?" Ben said before sitting down.

"Twin boys," Ellie answered, lovingly grasping his hand.

"Who'd have ever thought that at my age . . ." Ben said.

Doug reached for Mara's hand. Life at the homestead had come full circle since his brother Dan's death had left Ellie a young widow. So much of both their lives had played out here in this place by the river where the two of them had first fallen in love. Finally, after years of feeling lost, everything felt right with his life. As Mara looked up at him and smiled, he knew she was the reason. Never again would he let anything come between them.

"I'm gonna babysit," Anna announced to the chuckles of everyone there. "Momma said I can be in charge when she and Ben need to go to the store sometimes—later, when the babies get bigger—you know, after they're born, of course."

"You're the perfect person for the job," Mara told her, smiling at the way Anna was already embracing her new brothers. She had been a lovely child and she was obviously going to be a lovely young lady.

"Thanks, Aunt Mara, maybe you can help me sometime when you're not on your boat."

"And what am I, chopped liver?" Doug teased.

"I meant you, too, Uncle Doug," she scowled. "C'mon, Thor. Let's go look for your ball."

By evening, when Joe and Sal had not yet arrived, Mara called Joe on his cell phone, concerned when she only got his voicemail. It was around 9 p.m. when Ben was the first to see him drive up.

"Did you have trouble finding us? I should have flown you in," Ben said after introducing himself and shaking the old man's hand.

"Had some complications with my wife," Joe said, "but my niece is staying with her and so I didn't want to miss such an important event as this . . ."

Joe's voice trailed off as he was introduced to each of the guests in turn, finally spotting Mara as she came out the kitchen door. He hurried over to see her.

"Where's Sal?" Mara asked him.

"She's home."

"Home?"

"She's been acting strange, Mara, ever since solstice and maybe even before. I don't know what to make of it."

"What do you mean by strange? I mean, I obviously know about the skiff incident, but is there more?" Mara asked.

"I don't know. Kind of preoccupied, I guess. She was planning to be here as of this morning and then right as I was leaving, she suddenly decided she couldn't take the time to leave the new business. It's not like her to act this way. Something's wrong, but I just don't know what it is."

Mara hugged the obviously concerned elder, feeling something jab her lightly when she did. When she stepped back, she saw the feather that Joe had given her so long ago still sticking out of the pocket of the jacket she had tucked it into on the day of her wedding.

"I see you wore your good suit today," she smiled.

Joe's face flushed slightly as he tucked the feather back down into his pocket. He seldom dressed in anything other than jeans, a shirt, and some kind of jacket, and Mara suspected that this "good suit" was one he saved for special occasions like weddings, funerals, and celebrations.

"I'm thinking that having the feather with you is some kind of sign, Joe—like maybe this time you need its special presence to protect you."

"Could be," Joe answered in his usual monotone.

"Did you notice that the red dot came back?" Mara asked.

"That's weird," Joe answered, taking the feather out to confirm the presence of a small red dot painted on the outer curved edge about a third of the way down. "What we got going on this time?"

Chapter Seven
New York

Elzianne LaMonte flipped her ermine jacket and matching bag onto the desk of her personal secretary as she walked into the suite of offices where she worked.

"I'll take care of that right away, Ms. LaMonte," the middle-aged woman said.

"Clear my appointments for this morning, Julia. And see if Mr. Drewstone can see me before noon."

"Right away, Ms. LaMonte," Julia Bruce said, as she adjusted the hair clip that was holding her tight chignon.

By 10:30 a.m., Elzi LaMonte had already reviewed a dozen pages of archival data with Harding Drewstone, president and CEO of the New York Cultural Museum.

"I apologize for the lack of a formal presentation on this information," she told him, "but Julia assures me she can have it all ready in time for the board meeting this evening."

By 3:30 p.m., she had finished presenting her findings to the board, and by 4 p.m., had received a firm commitment of three million dollars for the research and purchase of historically significant tsunami debris from Alaska.

"You will not be disappointed in the exhibit that this money will allow us to present to the public," she told them. "My source has ready access to all that we need, and that source, gentlemen, is someone whom I have known for a very long time."

The next morning, Elzianne LaMonte arrived in her office at precisely the same time as she did every day—7:45 a.m.—and flipped the same ermine jacket with its same matching bag onto the desk of the woman who had served as her personal assistant for the past thirty years.

"As soon as things open up in Alaska—about four hours from now—please secure plane fare and accommodations for twelve to Hoonah, Alaska. And plan on spending the rest of summer up there with me and the rest of the crew," Elzianne commanded.

"But—well—excuse me, Ms. LaMonte—I'm sure that with all that's going on that you may have forgotten that my only daughter is getting married in mid-July of this year—"

"She'll have to change it, Julia—or get married without her mommy being there. Now, make sure that the rooms are decent and at least have plumbing. It's a god-forsaken place up there. And we're all going to need those pants the hillbillies all wear. What do they call them—carhats or hearts or something? We're all going to need those pants and some warm jackets and, for crying out loud, do make sure we all have some decent footwear. I didn't see a stitch of pavement the entire time I was up there."

Julia tightened her jaw, reached back and adjusted the clip holding her chignon, brushed the wrinkles from the lap of her Chanel suit, and shifted almost imperceptibly in her chair before looking—as if for the first time—directly at the departing figure of the woman she had worked for her entire adult life.

Through everything in her past, she had been as loyal as any personal assistant could be. Through her own marriage, the birth of her only child, a divorce, a bankruptcy scandal, and a cancer scare, she had reported to work every day exactly one hour before her boss's arrival and had never once spoken a harsh or negative word to the woman who paid her twice what she would make elsewhere, and who afforded her first-class access to the finest shopping and dining facilities in New York.

But today, well paid as she was, would be the last day that Julia stood by as Elzianne LaMonte relegated her needs to the level of the bathroom tissue she so meticulously replaced with a fresh full roll every time her boss used the restroom.

At exactly 4:25 p.m. New York time, she handed her boss an itemized list confirming full travel and lodging accommodations for the entire upcoming summer, as well as receipts guaranteeing timely delivery of outdoor wear for each of those who would be traveling to Hoonah for the summer.

Then, stepping through the door, she bade her employer her usual good evening, before abruptly turning back to face her, speaking in soft, definitive tones that left no doubt about the depth of her resolve.

"I think you will find my desk in order and each of my assigned tasks either fully completed or with clear instructions as to how to finish them. I have taken the liberty of arranging to have my departing check sent to my home as I would find it next to unbearable to have to listen to your suffering voice or gaze into your pitiless eyes ever again."

With that, Julia Evelyn Bruce stiffened her spine and walked briskly out the door, leaving Elzianne LaMonte staring at the empty space beneath her ermine that had been occupied for thirty years by the only person who had ever been loyal to her.

Chapter Eight
Inside Information

S al got up from her recliner and threw another log in the woodstove. She looked at the matching chair where her husband usually sat, and set a fresh cup of tea on the small table she shared with him each morning. Mesmerized by the calm that the quiet, silky waters of Icy Strait brought over her, she basked in the warm comfort sipping the tea brought her from the constant drizzle that had left her feeling cold and alone since Joe had left for Palmer.

When the phone rang, she tried to ignore it, but what if it was Joe, and what if something was wrong? She picked it up and heard her niece begin to speak.

"I just got done cleaning the last of the rooms over at the lodge and I heard someone at the desk talking about a group of people from New York coming in to stay near that salvage place run by some guy they called *Hoonah Joe* and some woman they didn't name. I think they were talking about your place, Aunt Sal."

"Hell's afire, Della, can't she just leave me alone?"

"I thought you'd be happy, Aunt Sal. I figured tourism would be good for the business," Della answered. "Besides, how'd you know it was a woman?"

"What'd be good fer the business would be if ya quit cleanin' fer other people and came to work fer me and yer Uncle Joe as long as yer gonna spend the entire summer here in Hoonah," Sal answered, dodging Della's question about the woman.

"I know, Aunt Sal. I'll think about it. Gotta go. Love you."

Sal paced across the living room several times before getting herself another cup of tea and sitting back to watch the fog move in.

"She's probably renting half that new cruise ship lodge up the road at the old cannery site," she muttered. "Twelve people! Is she bringing danged TV cameras with her, too? She doesn't seem to do much of anything without a blast of publicity surrounding it."

She shifted in her chair and watched the fog creep along the horizon. Maybe their paths wouldn't cross that much, especially with hers and Joe's operation being in the opposite direction just before the airport. She shouldn't be over-reacting this way. Hadn't she managed to shield herself from her toxic relationship with Elzi for all these years? Sure, this was a bit too close for comfort and totally out of the blue, but Elzi could hurt her only if she let her. She was strong enough now and she would choose to rise above all this. Besides, Elzi would quickly tire of Alaska and be gone out of her hair soon enough, anyway. She shifted again in her chair, raised the footrest, and sipped some more tea.

And what was with all this *Hoonah Joe*? Who had come up with *that* one? Treating her Joey like some kind of cheap tourist attraction. She'd *Hoonah Joe* Elzianne LaMonte if she ever did cross paths with her, which she fervently hoped would not happen, just as she full well knew that it was inevitable.

Nice that Della had tipped her off. Maybe it was good that Joe's niece was working at the lodge after all. It would be a good way to keep an eye on her sister without her even knowing about it. She made a mental note to discuss the matter with Della later. She wouldn't tell her too much—like the very fact that Elzianne was her sister. She'd say that she was an old acquaintance from college—no, not that! No one in her current life knew she had ever gone to college. No, she would simply say Elzianne was someone she worked with as a young woman, many, many years ago.

That's what she'd tell Joe—and Mara and Doug, too, except she would also tell them that Elzianne had gotten into some legal trouble back then, causing her to distance herself from the woman who had once been her friend.

For her part, she would be cordial, but wary. Elzianne LaMonte was about as welcome to Sal's world in Hoonah as a case of shingles and plague combined.

When the phone rang again, it was Joe. His voice sounded lighter when she told him she was feeling better and admitted that maybe she should have made the trip to Palmer. She'd meet him at the airport the next morning.

"I love you, too, sweet baby," she told him before hanging up.

Maybe keeping the truth about Elzi from him was wrong, but the woman was so evil that it was all she could think of to do to protect the man she loved.

Chapter Nine
Switched after Birth

When she picked Joe up the next morning, Sal filled him in on Della's job at the hotel as well as the news about the group that would be descending on them for the remainder of the summer. She almost felt like her old self again when they shared a laugh about his new *Hoonah Joe* moniker. When she told him that a troubled old friend from her past named Elzianne LaMonte would be spending the rest of the summer in Hoonah and it brought no more response than a nod of his head, her stomach churned just a tad less intensely than she had expected it to.

"The kids will be coming in tomorrow," Joe told her, referring to Doug and Mara by the affectionate name he had taken to calling them. "The good news is that they're planning on spending the rest of the summer right here in Hoonah."

"What's goin' on with that, Joey?" Sal asked.

"What do you mean? I thought you'd be happy about that. Don't be getting all suspicious now, Sal."

"I ain't suspicious now and I ain't plannin' on bein' suspicious then," Sal barked. "Although the way ya all been dotin' on me woulda drove a lesser woman right around the bend and halfway down the next two roads a life what with all the danged 'help' yer hell bent on providin' ta me."

"They're planning on helping out with the shop, or whatever you need 'em for, and just being here to spend some time with us. They went to a lot of personal trouble and expense to do it, too, Sal, so—well, just so you know, that's all."

"Well, I love 'em dearly and ya danged well know that, Joey, but hell's afire, ain't I got enough on my plate already what with getting' the business goin'— and Della's showed up, and now Mara and her ole man . . ."

"Why do you keep referring to Doug by everything except the name he was given at birth?" Joe said, taking her aback.

She stood up without answering and took her time, pretending to stretch while she waited to see what her husband would say next. She could count on two fingers the times that Joe had ever questioned her about anything, much less criticized her. When he remained silent, she bent over and picked up his empty teacup and carried it to the kitchen, still waiting for him to say something—anything.

"I asked you a question, Sal. Now come on over here and sit back down and let's talk about this."

Suddenly the tears came as Sal scrunched a dishtowel and held it to her eyes. Still her husband said nothing. After about fifteen minutes of the hardest sobs she had experienced in years, she quietly sat down in her own chair next to her husband's and poured out the details of her past, including Elzianne's attempts to implicate her deceased husband, Bert, in wrongdoing at the bank in their hometown.

"I don't talk much about Bert, Joey. I figure it ain't no interest to you to hear about my ex and he's dead anyway, so what the . . ."

Sal dabbed her eyes as Joe sat looking dumbfounded. For the longest time he said nothing.

"Are you going to respond to what I just told you, or have I misjudged your willingness to accept the truth about my past?" Sal said, using the perfect diction that reflected her privileged upbringing.

Suddenly Joe jumped up from his chair.

"I don't know what's going on with you Sal. I've never seen you this way. Part of me wonders if you're getting Alzheimer's or dementia, or who knows what, and part of me just sits here in disbelief that I married a woman who isn't even who I thought she was."

"I can understand why you'd feel that way, Joey," Sal said. "A huge voice inside me didn't even want to tell you about this. I had to, though. Our life together is all that matters to me. Trust me—believe me when I tell you that the day I stopped being Sylvia LaMonte Kindle, and just became Sal, was the happiest, truest, most meaningful day of my life."

After Joe Michael strode silently to the door, letting it slam behind him, Sylvia LaMonte crumpled to the floor and sobbed uncontrollably.

Chapter Ten
Are You Kidding Me?

S al was asleep on the floor when Mara found her the next day.
"Sal? Joe? We're back," she called as she let herself in. "Doug's putting our things in the guest cabin. It's sure nice of you two to let us—"

"Jane? That you?" Sal said sleepily, thankful that her persona as Sal Kindle had become second nature to her.

"What are you doing on the floor, Sal? Where's Joe? What's wrong? Have you been crying? Where's Joe, Sal? Is it his heart again?"

Mara rushed to help the old woman up and then ran to the door.

"Doug! Doug! C'mere. Hurry!"

"What's going on?" Doug asked, trying to figure out what was happening.

"Joe's gone and Sal was sleeping here on the floor. Something's wrong," Mara answered.

"It's not what ya think, Jane," Sal said.

"Well, then, what is it, Sal?" Doug said, growing impatient with all the confusion surrounding the old woman as of late.

"Make me some tea, would ya, Jane? I'll explain, but first let me use the restroom and get ma wits about me."

Doug built a fire in the woodstove while Mara helped Sal clean up and find some fresh clothes.

"Are you hurt anywhere, Sal? A woman your age can't be sleeping on the floor all night in this kind of weather. Don't worry about the tea. Doug's making it."

"How many times've I told ya that I ain't no pansy, Jane? That bear rug was as soft and toasty as any bed I been in, and that wool blanket and a coupla sofa pillows was all I needed to be toasty warm."

"What's going on, Sal? Where's Joe?" Mara asked.

Sal looked at her feet and didn't answer. Instead, she pulled her sweater tightly around her and walked back to the kitchen where Doug was just finishing making the tea.

"Joe said I gotta stop callin' ya by everythin' but yer given name," she said, looking sheepishly up at Doug. "Guess he's right, huh—Doug? Thanks fer the tea."

Doug pulled a chair out for Sal, glancing at Mara as he did.

"You can call me anything you want to, Sal, but just tell us where Joe is and what's going on."

"I dunno," Sal said. "I never seen him this mad."

"Mad?"

"Yup. Mad as a hornet," Sal answered.

"But, why?" Mara asked.

Sal stared into her teacup for what seemed like hours. Finally, she looked up at Mara and then Doug, took one of their hands into each of her own and began talking in a manner that completely blew them away.

"You know me as Sal Kindle, widow of Bert Kindle, and wife of Joe Michael," she began.

Why was she talking this way—perfectly, softly, and with the utmost display of propriety that either of them had ever seen?

"What must be obvious to you both by now is that I am more than the woman named Sal that you both know."

Sal chuckled lightly, resuming a serious tone when they sat stone-faced and didn't respond.

"My real name is Sylvia Anna Lorraine LaMonte. I was born in Rhinebeck, New York, raised by—well, raised by a series of perfectly programmed nannies, went to Yale, married an investment banker named Bert Kindle, and moved with him to Alaska to escape a growing litany—if you will—of trumped-up embezzlement and insider-trading charges brought against Bert by my younger sister, Elzianne, and by my own mother."

"Are you talking about Elzianne LaMonte, the society matron, who divorced her husband when she found out he was gay, and then was sued by him for support?" Mara asked.

"One and the same, Mara," Sal answered, calling Mara by her given name—something she rarely did. "How did you know about her?"

"It was in all the tabloids and on all the talk shows," Mara answered. "I think I saw something on the TV while I was working at KonaJane's a while back."

"Elzianne LaMonte is my sister and she's—well, it's complicated, but let's just say that she's been here once and is coming back to spend the rest of the summer in her role as director of a museum in New York."

"Wow," Doug said. "You mean that she's been here—right here in Hoonah? So what does that mean for you? And why is Joe gone?"

"That's right, Doug. She was here solstice weekend. I ran into her when I went to the *Beachmopper* to get more supplies. That's what we named the landing craft, you know—*Beachmopper*."

Sal took a long sip of her tea and quietly stared out the window.

"Being anywhere near Elzianne is never good for me," Sal continued. "I thought I had freed myself from her forever by moving to Alaska and changing everything about who I was, but fate brought us together on that remote stretch of beach and now that she's found me, well . . ."

"Can't you just ignore her? Wait for her to leave?" Mara asked.

"I wish I could," Sal replied. "But she's already clued me in that now that she's found me, there will be a rough road ahead for me, and for anything and everyone attached to me."

"Well, she can't change the way we feel about you," Doug said, jumping up from his chair.

"She's already insinuated that she's trying to stir up more trouble to implicate Bert, only, instead of turning our mother against me, she's persuaded our nephew—a young lawyer—to investigate Bert's death."

"What do you mean?" Mara asked.

"I mean that she's going to try to build a case that either Bert's death was no accident or that he took his own life, implicating me—his sole heir—well, let's just say negatively," Sal answered.

"And Joe knows all this?" Doug asked.

"No," Sal answered. "He only knows my real identity. He left before I could explain. I guess the shock of it all upset him more than I thought it would."

Sal sipped her tea and let Doug and Mara absorb what she had said.

"I need to warn you both that I believe that Elzi's going to start with trying to get both the *Driftfeather* and the *StormRoamer*," Sal said. "You remember that I told you that Bert and I bought them together, don't you?"

Mara looked at Doug, who had turned as white as a sheet.

"Everything I have is tied up in those seiners," he said so softly that Mara had to strain to hear him.

"But she's not going to stop there," Sal continued. "Before she's done with me, she'll have everything Joe and I own and more, including everything we find from the tsunami debris."

"Oh, Sal," Mara said. "I don't know what to say."

"Nothin' ta say, Jane," Sal said, reverting to the persona they all knew. "Jest look out fer ma Joey fer me fer a while."

Sal laughed and got up to pour herself another cup of tea. When she returned, she spoke as Sylvia LaMonte.

"I need to return to New York and find a way to prove that my sister has done everything I just told you. You see, before it was enough for me to just move away, but now, well, now I have Joe to think about and as I live and breathe, Elzianne LaMonte will rue the day she ever does one single thing to hurt Joe Michael."

Just then the door slammed and Joe Michael walked in.

"Did she tell you what she told me—that she's not who we all thought she was?" he said, obviously still angry.

"That and more, Joe," Doug answered. "I think you need to hear her out, Joe. Sal loves you and you love her and, well, I know this is all a shock—to all of us—but once you hear the full story, I think you'll feel differently."

Everyone watched as Joe Michael paced the room. None of them had ever seen him this angry except for the time he had confronted an evil criminal that threatened to harm his family. Quietly, they watched him pace until, looking more dejected than angry, he finally sat down at the table to join them.

Joe Michael placed his weathered hand on top of Sal's as one, then two tears rolled down his cheeks. "I think I do, too," he said softly, squeezing Sal's hand. "I think so, too."

Chapter Eleven
Sixty-Some Years ago on Christmas Day

J oe Michael had been more understanding than any man ever known to Sylvia LaMonte would have been in similar circumstances. When this was all over, could she return to him as the Sal Kindle that he loved? Her heart begged for it to be so. Their marriage, after all, had been legal, with Sylvia having used the initials of her real name to have it legally changed to Sal long before she met the wonderful man she now called her husband. And their love—well, that was real, too.

They had reminded each other of that love at the airport before she left a week after he had learned her real identity and the story that went with it. Joe had even offered to accompany her to Rhinebeck, though he knew this was something that she would have to do alone. If there was a battle to be fought at this stage in her life, she would make sure that its main focus would be to hold on to her life with Joe Michael.

~ ~ ~

When she arrived in Rhinebeck a week later, Sylvia LaMonte found that things hadn't changed much around the old estate or around the neighboring estates that had been her childhood world. When she later stumbled upon a stooped and frail-looking old man sitting on a park bench in the church cemetery, she was shocked to recognize him as her high school sweetheart, John Thomas St. Jean.

"So, you left me for this church and it is at this church where I now find you all these years later, J.T.," Sylvia LaMonte said softly.

At first he didn't reply, choosing instead to lift his eyes briefly to meet hers. It was enough for her to see the flicker of recognition that told her he remembered her, so she sat on the bench beside him and took his gnarled, trembling hand into her own and sat silently beside him.

"I guess you should call me Monsignor now, Sylvia," he said, patting her hand with his free one, while slipping his other one free.

"Monsignor?" Sylvia answered. "Right here at St. Aloysius?"

"Yes," he answered. "Monsignor."

"It was right here, right on this very bench, I believe, that you told me you were leaving for the seminary," Sylvia said softly. "Right here—on Christmas Day nearly sixty years ago."

She stood up, faced him and said, "And you've never left?"

"The family arranged things to keep me here," he answered. "I didn't think about it. I knew them all. This was my home. Why should I think of leaving? The people here needed one of their own. Someone talked to the Archbishop, donations were made, and next thing I knew, I was assigned to St. Aloysius and that never changed."

"I see," Sylvia answered.

"And don't get me wrong, Sylvia, I have no regrets. My life is as I wanted it to be and my service to God meant as much to me here as it could have or would have anywhere else. The challenges here, although they may have seemed simplistic, were immense, but God's will prevailed and I was able to maintain purity of direction even amongst the underlying chaos that you—having been raised here—understand all too well."

Sylvia stared at two clouds sailing lazily across the blue sky. A flock of birds swooped in synchrony from one tree to another and then back to the first tree again.

"If anyone could have maintained rightness and equilibrium in the face of the circumstances that kept you against all odds in this one location for an entire lifetime, I would unhesitatingly say that it would be you, Monsignor," Sylvia said gently.

"It couldn't have been easy for you knowing that politics and favoritism carved your path. I know this and you know this and so there is no sense in mincing our words about that reality."

"You were always able to see past it all, Sylvia," Monsignor St. Jean replied. "I always admired that strength—envied it—even as I begged our Lord's forgiveness for holding that jealous thought within my heart."

"I can see that your life has not been as easy as it would appear," Sylvia continued.

"You have always understood," Monsignor St. Jean answered.

For the next long while the two sat there in silence, while Monsignor St. Jean silently prayed his rosary, moving his frail hands along the well-worn beads as his lips mouthed the words to the prayers, and Sylvia let her thoughts drift to the years long ago when they had sat on this very bench for the second to the last time.

He had been a man as kind as he had been handsome. Though their affection for each other had been true, she had known deep inside that they were destined for separate paths in life, and a parting that would be bittersweet.

"May I bless you before you leave?" Monsignor St. Jean said, his silhouette surrounded by the crimson evening sky.

Sylvia Anna Lorraine LaMonte returned to the present, lowered her head, and accepted the profound gift bestowed upon her by her long-ago friend. When she opened her eyes and looked up, Monsignor St. Jean's tired and aged form was moving in the direction of the setting sun, slowly and steadily and once more away.

Chapter Twelve
Rhinebeck

It was front-page news in Rhinebeck when two days later Monsignor St. Jean was found dead of natural causes in the church rectory.

One week later at his funeral, a young priest tapped Sylvia on her shoulder as she was leaving the church. After asking her for her full name, he handed her a mahogany box that was slightly larger than a shoebox and much more square, along with a court order stating that the box, the key and its point of access had been officially willed to her by Monsignor St. Jean.

She sat in the last pew of the church as she opened it. Inside was Monsignor St. Jean's rosary, a yellowed newspaper clipping about his graduation from the seminary and assignment to St. Aloysius, and a key. Engraved on the old-style key were the initials RSB and the number 7, which minimal research proved to belong to a safety deposit box at Rhinebeck State Bank.

Sylvia closed the lid on the box and tucked it under her arm, genuflecting for the first time in over sixty years as she left the church. By late afternoon, she had rented a cottage next to one of the old violet houses in the village, remembering the times she had visited this very location with her nanny to shop for violets for her mother.

The old greenhouse was now empty, its perimeter overgrown with grasses and the surviving perennials that had once been meticulously kept. She sat on one of the old cement park benches that had once provided respite for husbands waiting for their wives to shop, and even for ladies who desired a moment in the sun.

At the foot of the bench a tiny violet peeked through the grass, showing one dark purple bloom. Sylvia plucked it and held to her nose. The fragrance was the same as she remembered—strong, pure, and enticing; not at all like today's violets that lacked any fragrance at all.

For a moment she was a young girl again, frolicking in the gentle meadows strewn with the plentiful fieldstones, which many in the predepression era of the early 1900s had used to build their homes.

The old greenhouse had fieldstone walls that stood about four feet tall and were topped with wooden frames likely manufactured in one of the old mills, which still held most of the original panes of the wavy antique glass produced during those times.

Just as the violet houses had been a haven for her as a child, her nearness to this one enveloped her with momentary peace. Once back inside the cottage, she slid the mahogany box inside a pillowcase before tucking it under her clothing in the corner of her suitcase.

How kind of J.T. to have remembered her so fondly. She looked heavenward, sure that he felt her warm regard. Then she took off her shoes and climbed onto the bed for an afternoon nap. When she awoke, the sun was setting, so she dressed in her nightclothes and crawled under the sheets for the most restful sleep she had enjoyed in weeks.

A week later, she was back on a plane to Alaska, the mahogany box now also holding the sealed manila envelope and a yellowed and smaller tattered envelope addressed to Father St. Jean that she had found after inserting RSB key #7 into Monsignor St. Jean's safety-deposit box at Rhinebeck State Bank.

Once back in Hoonah she would sort through everything and try to understand why this man she had not had any contact with for over sixty years had chosen to leave her his meager belongings and whatever the envelopes from RSB box 7 contained. But for now, her Joey was waiting and she had a business to run with the busy tourist season almost in full swing.

In the fall she would return to Rhinebeck if necessary, or maybe just to smell the violets now gone wild.

Chapter Thirteen
Back in Hoonah

"Sal's back," Della shouted as she breezed through the door of Beachmoppers on her way to work. "See ya later, Uncle Joe."

Joe Michael raced across town, forgetting the load of trash he had stuffed into the bed of his dualie, which now left a trail of loose papers and cardboard behind him.

"You're back sooner 'n I thought you'd be," he said. "Why did ya go and take a cab anyway? Why didn't you just call me or Mara or Doug to—"

Sal threw her arms around him, kissing him fully on the lips.

"You know that there's nothing in Rhinebeck that could keep me away very long," she said, surprising even herself at the way her childhood diction had returned, and causing Joe to momentarily raise one eyebrow at the sound of her voice.

"Della says that Elzi and her entourage arrived yesterday," he said, stepping back to pull out a chair for his wife at the table near the window where they usually had lunch. After he had seated her, he sat in his own chair right across from her. "Come to think of it, there's been a bunch of city people wandering into the business for the last day or so."

"Ya can spot 'em a mile away in all those brand-new outdoor catalog clothes," Sal laughed.

The sandwiches that Mara had dropped off for Joe earlier were wonderful. When they had finished eating, they lingered in their familiar places, sitting silently with each gazing at the peaceful grayness of the ocean.

"I guess I could just sit here all day if I let myself," Sal said wistfully, before getting up to take the dirty dishes to the sink.

"There's no better place on earth," Joe agreed, before pushing himself away from the table that Sal had just wiped down before carrying her bag to the laundry room and emptying its contents into the washer.

"I still can't believe you didn't call one of us to pick you up," Joe said.

"Hell's afire, Joey, ya know and I know how danged busy you are this time a year. Don'tcha think that's why God made cabs?"

"It's hard for me to believe that you have another side to you, Sal," Joe laughed. "In spite of that swanky accent you're sayin' is the real you, you still sound just like the woman I fell in love with and married up here in Alaska."

"That's because I am the woman ya fell in love with and married, Joe. There ain't nothin' about that that's changed one iota. Besides, ya never know when that highfalutin' accent I grew up with will come in handy. Now how about some nice hot tea and I'll fill you in on my time in Rhinebeck."

Chapter Fourteen
Showtime

Elzi LaMonte, her every move captured by a young man with a large video camera, stooped to pick up an item off one the tables inside Beachmoppers.

"May I handle it?" she said to Mara, who had followed the entourage to see what was going on.

"Well, I mean—yes—of course," Mara stuttered.

"Don't fret, dear, I'll use due care," Elzi snipped.

Elzi paused dramatically, her long silk scarf sweeping the tops of the goods that the table bore, before reaching for a glass fishing float that was an unusual color of opalescent gray. She held it up to capture the light, turning it slowly with the tips of her fingers, as the cameraman stepped closer and zoomed in on her face, her hands, and then on Mara's face.

"Tell me what you know about it. What you think its value is?" Elzi said, turning her back to put the float back down on the table before Mara could answer.

When she turned back around, Doug Williams was staring down at her from his place in front of his wife.

"I'm sorry ma'am, but we do not allow photographers inside Beachmoppers for security purposes," he said in a firm, but gentlemanly voice, as he placed the palm of one hand in front of the camera lens to stop the filming.

"There was no sign, young man. Is the manager here? I mean, surely that would not be you, now, would it? Someone, so—so—I don't know, someone so—uh—obviously—well, no need to insult you."

Doug did not shrink back the way Elzi had expected him to. In her years of perfecting her dismissive demeanor, she had seldom encountered anyone who would not immediately back off when she squared her shoulders, lifted her chin, and issued whatever directive—whether succinctly stated or inferred—she issued.

"I'm the danged manager, owner, proprietor, and the hell-fired end a your snoopin' around ma business, Elzianne LaMonte," Sal interrupted, walking up to face her sister full on. "And git that danged camera offa ma face ya little twerp," she said, brushing the camera with one hand while leaning on the table with her other.

"Oh, Sylvia, you have so deftly managed that colloquial little accent to the point that a body would almost believe you came from right here at the end of all things civilized," Elzianne said coolly.

"I don't know who you are or why you have decided to come all the way to Hoonah to terrorize my wife, ma'am," Joe Michael said evenly, stepping out from behind a partition near the table. His voice was soft and low with its monotonic accent belying the anger that was overtaking his normally gentle nature. "But you need to understand that the fact that I'm standing here talking to you at all would be viewed by just about anybody who knows me as a clear sign that you are going somewhere with your highfalutin' pushiness that you will live to regret."

"Take it easy, now, Joe," Doug said, stepping forward and placing a hand on Joe Michael's shoulder. "Let me—"

Joe jerked his shoulder away from Doug in a rare display of defiance. "Not this time, Doug. This time, I'll take care of—"

"Excuse me, Sir. Are you threatening me? Somebody call Dorland," Elzi said, waving her arm in a dramatic sweep that sent her staff into an apparently well-rehearsed clamor to please her.

"I think it's best if you leave," Mara said, trying to smooth the rapidly escalating confrontation.

"No one, nobody, throws Elzianne Jeanette LaMonte out of anywhere!" Elzi hissed.

"That's not what the danged tabloids said, Elzi. Now get movin' afore I call the law," Sal bellowed.

Mara dared not breathe until she heard the huge wooden door to Beachmoppers thump closed. No one said anything as the few remaining tourists hurried toward the exit. Sal actually left the room, followed quickly by Joe Michael, leaving her and Doug to busy themselves straightening tables before finally following suit.

By the next morning, Doug had hammered up a large sign that read: *No cameras. We reserve the right to refuse service to anyone,* and Mara had designed and printed up handouts outlining rules of conduct—including a ban on cameras—for those choosing to visit Beachmoppers.

Chapter Fifteen
Reflection

When the cruise ship pulled out the next morning, Joe, Sal, Mara, and Doug all waved as if in some desperate attempt to regain the goodwill of the passengers who had all but abandoned Beachmoppers after their confrontation with Elzi.

Doug had done his best at damage control by meeting with the cruise director to explain some of the circumstances of the altercation—an effort he polished by providing 10 percent discounts to all of that cruise line's passengers for the remainder of the season.

"I ain't one ta suck up ta the touri, Doug," Sal sputtered. "Danged, nosy, meddlin', no-good-enough-ta-even-earn-the-name-a-sister, dysfunctional excuse fer a relative . . ."

"What's wrong with Aunt Sal?" Della asked her uncle.

Joe Michael took his niece by the arm and led her out to his dualie.

"How about if we go out for some coffee and I'll try to explain," he told her. When he reached for his truck keys, he felt the feather brush against his thumb.

For just an instant, tears welled in his eyes as the significance of the feather came into his consciousness. This situation, everything that had been going on with Sal, had to be more than a simple family feud or why else would he have been given the feather? He was as tired of all the drama as everyone else he was close to had become. At his advanced age, could he even handle another battle?

He reached for the feather again. He felt its softness held together by the quill's strong spine. Mara had given it to him. What did *that* mean? Hadn't he been the one who had first given it to her—a protector sent to cross paths with her by some unknown destiny. Mara, once a stranger and now like a daughter to him—perhaps even somehow sent to him by a greater power—now protecting him.

It was not as though it was the first time she had done so. There had been many instances when he had known that their destinies were entwined, starting back when her father had risked his life to save him in the Vietnam War, and later leading to his own promise on that friend's deathbed that he would always look out for her.

He steered the dualie into the parking lot of the local coffee shop, automatically putting it in park before walking around to open the door for Della. If nothing else, Joe Michael was a gentleman to all who knew him.

"Well, do you, Uncle Joe?" Della asked, squinting her eyes and cocking her head to try to force an answer.

"Do I what, Della?" Joe said, his thoughts snapping back to the present.

"Do you think that Aunt Sal is going to be okay, what with her sister giving her so much trouble and all that?" Della asked. Hadn't he understood the question the first two times she had asked it?

Still, Joe Michael didn't answer. Instead, taking Della by the arm, he led her inside.

Something was wrong, and Della chose not to push the matter.

"I'll have regular black coffee," Joe told their server.

"And a shot-in-the-dark for me," Della said.

"That's funny, the way coffee comes with names now," Joe laughed.

Della rolled her eyes before patting the old man on the hand with one hand while scrolling through the texts on her smartphone with the other.

"I gotta be at work in an hour," she announced. "And Mara says to send you over to Beachmoppers if I find you."

Joe watched as Della used both thumbs to type her replies. Her arm had healed well enough to allow her such use. He looked heavenward and said a silent thank you that she had recovered from the horrible ambush that had left her arm nearly destroyed by the gunshot of a conscienceless outlaw.

He had settled that score by capturing the young man who was so evil that he had gunned down his own father before Joe's eyes. A trial had convicted the murderer and a judge had sentenced him to life in prison with no opportunity for parole. Two appeals had failed in the courts already, and Joe Michael was certain that Carlos Antoya would never again hurt Della or anyone else, for that matter. For the good man, Santiago, whose love Carlos had repaid with death, Joe again looked heavenward and thanked God for justice.

"There's something I need to tell you, Della," Joe Michael began.

Forty-five minutes later, Della got up, kissed the old man on the forehead, and walked across the street to work.

Chapter Sixteen
Blue Pottery

Things returned to normal at Beachmoppers a few days after the confrontation with Elzianne. Perhaps it was because no one had seen her around town—a fact verified when Della informed Mara that Elzi and her entourage had flown out with a private pilot the day before.

"I'm not sure where they went," she told Sal later, "but I did hear something about checking the coastline by air."

Meanwhile, Joe and Sal's teams continued to bring in items they salvaged from the coastline, including a couple of pieces of broken pottery that had been found scattered around a perfectly intact rectangular piece that was about twelve inches square and eight inches deep that they decided was some kind of planter.

Sal left it sitting on the stoop after deciding that it probably would only bring in a few dollars. She said she wasn't sure, so she left it there until she could make up her mind whether to keep it or not.

Seeing it sitting there for several days, Joe filled it with water when he saw Thor lying next to it in the hot sun one afternoon, and from that day on, it became the wolf-dog's personal outdoor water bowl.

"I guess it might as well get some use," Sal said, shrugging her shoulders when she saw it.

"I think it gives Beachmoppers more of a rustic, antique feel," Mara said. "It just looks kind of old, you know. Gee, I hope it's not radioactive or anything."

"Didn't even think of that," Joe said.

Doug immediately dumped the water, and then grabbed the Geiger counter they had purchased for the business and went over the old container just to make sure. Although officials had often tried to reassure the public that none of the tsunami debris from the huge earthquake in Japan could be radioactive, few believed that to be true, so Sal had purchased the Geiger counter to check everything, just to be safe. When Doug detected nothing unusual after scanning Thor's dish, he set it back down next to the bench and filled it with fresh water.

Mara filled the old water bucket with petunias a few days later and set that next to the bench behind Thor's new bowl, noticing that something about the pale blue color of the water bowl seemed to acquire a new depth once the flowers were beside it for contrast.

"I'm glad we decided to keep it," she told Sal, taking her outside to show her the arrangement. "I really love this old pottery. Pretty interesting that it got over here without being broken, too."

The other pieces of pottery they had found had been more ornate, carrying complicated patterns in bright shades of red and gold. None of them had survived intact.

"Too bad those got broken instead of this old ordinary thing," Sal had said. "It's jest like everything else, the cheap stuff always holds up way longer than ya ever dreamed possible or wanted to have it hangin' around. Guess it's good enough for Thor's water dish though."

Chapter Seventeen
Settling In

Two more cruise ships came and went without incident, and business at Beachmoppers was brisk, with many people taking advantage of the 10 percent discount offered to the cruise lines.

Sal's landing craft crews were staying busy, bringing in a full load weekly—enough to keep a sorting crew on two daily shifts out in the yard. Floats were the biggest sellers, especially those that contained Japanese lettering. It was reassuring to the tourists that each piece was marked "tested and found negative for radioactivity," a concern that seemed to be universally shared.

Driftwood was another popular item, but not as much as pieces of painted wood that had once belonged to the personal homes and belongings of actual Japanese people. For those items, Sal had set up a fund where 50 percent of the proceeds would go directly to the people of Japan, and then only if the original owners could not be found so that the item could be returned directly to them.

Once, they had even found a small box filled with personal items and inscribed with someone's name. The Japanese consul in Juneau was able to locate that person, whose entire family had perished in the earthquake. The box of items contained the only memories she had left, including a locket with the only remaining picture of her parents inside. The return of the box had astounded the young owner and given her strength when she needed it most.

"No! I don't wanna be interviewed fer no danged news story," Sal insisted, when reporters contacted her about the story. "We found it, we gave it back, it was the decent thing ta do. Scavengin' is scavengin', but even us scrap pickers has gotta line we ain't crossin' fer fame or fer money."

Business was also good at sea, with Derrk Stanley reporting that both the *Driftfeather* and the *Storm Roamer* were bringing in record catches to a highly competitive international demand for wild Alaska seafood. Mara heard Doug tell Derrk how relieved he was to hear that news. Doug had been worried about taking advantage of his friend, and now he could relax and concentrate on helping out in Hoonah.

The summer was a good one, too, with more than the usual number of clear, sunny days—days that found Thor often sleeping outside beside his new water bowl, lifting his head occasionally to sniff the petunias that had grown into a splendid trail beside it, rolling over every few hours to stretch, and maybe even getting up to take a drink, before falling asleep in the sun again.

Joe Michael had found his niche, too. He spent his mornings ferrying items back and forth between the work yard and Beachmoppers, and his afternoons greeting the tourists who seemed to have an insatiable appetite for talking with a real Alaska Native elder.

Joe talked of the history of Hoonah and of the bears, otters, deer, and sea mammals that inhabited the area. Once in a while he could be seen walking among the rows of photographers, who often sat with their huge-lensed cameras mounted on tripods along the beach, pointing to the many totems on Graveyard Island.

Mara stopped her usual brisk walk by at the sight of Joe talking to them on the beach one day. Was he showing some of them the feather? The photographers were paying no more than a polite interest in the feather, though. Still, how unusual for Joe to be so open like this.

She asked him about it one day.

"I can't really say why I took it out like I did," he told her. "Maybe I figured talking about it would help to make some sense out of why it keeps coming around. They didn't care, though," he laughed wryly. "It's just a feather and all they wanted to know was if it was from an eagle, or if it had magical or healing powers. I told 'em I couldn't say that for sure and so they just went on to somethin' else."

"Does it bother you to have the feather again?" Mara asked him.

"Bother me? Like a hangnail," Joe laughed.

He took on a serious tone. "It was me that gave it to you and since then it has taken on its own path, its own journey. I am left wondering if it is following destiny or if it is creating or even altering destiny. So, I guess the answer is yes, the feather troubles me. It troubles me because I don't understand it anymore. When it was protecting you, I understood it, but now that it has returned to me, I don't understand it anymore. Yes, it troubles me, Mara. It troubles me."

Mara took the feather from the old man's hand and tucked it into his breast pocket.

"You must allow life to unfold in its own way," she told him. "That is one lesson that the feather taught me."

She watched Joe's face and saw his puzzled expression momentarily shift to the hint of a smile.

"Your father would be proud of the woman you've become," he told her. "He'd be every bit as proud as I am, for sure."

Chapter Eighteen
Once Again, Goodbye

S al left so unexpectedly one August morning, that Joe barely had time to
finish his morning coffee before getting her to the airport.

"I can come with you now or I can come later," he told her. "Just say the
word and I'll be there."

"No sense, Joey. No sense troublin' you with this mess any more'n I have
already," she answered, using a mix of both her childhood and her colloquial accents.

"How long will you be, do you think?" he asked her.

"Well, hard ta say," she replied. "I'd like ta take that weaselin' little twerp,
Dorland and show 'im the business side a ma rifle," she sputtered, sounding
more like the Sal that Joe had married.

Then she sighed, took a deep breath, and said with perfect diction,
"Dorland Kindle is a puppet controlled by Elzianne, Joe. There's a reason
that his father and my Bert were as estranged as any two brothers can be.
Everyone in Rhinebeck knows that both Dorland and his father, Driscoll,
wanted to get their hands on Bert's estate when he died, but in spite of all
the legal challenges they mounted, none of their shenanigans worked. They
didn't work when they tried to horn in on Bert's business dealings when he
was alive either. They never cared a hoot about Bert, only about his money
and his long list of contacts.

Now that Dorland's old man has passed on, it looks like the son will follow
the father and do everything he can to vilify Bert Kindle, and the good name
he carried all his life."

"Couldn't you just let your lawyer handle all this?" Joe asked her.

Sal smiled and reached her hand over to lay it on top of Joe's.

"You are such a kind man, Joe Michael. Why should I be at all surprised to hear you talk this way, to assume that this is a simple matter that can be resolved with civility and decorum? You wouldn't know of the ways of people like Dorland Kindle and his father. People whose only path in life is on the backs of those they can use."

"I've seen my share of evil," Joe answered.

"There's no denying that you have," Sal said. "But people like Dorland and Driscoll Kindle, and Bert's father, Jameson, before them, take evil to a whole new level. It is one thing to be conned and swindled in life, but it is quite another to be so defiled in the name of love, honesty, and family loyalty. That, my wonderful husband, is a special kind of evil."

Joe and Sal embraced tightly before he walked her to the plane. He kissed her on the cheek and helped her up the three stairs to her seat in the tail section of the small plane that held fifteen people excluding the pilot and copilot.

He stood by the plane with his hand on the door while the pilot finished loading the luggage and did a full walk-around to check that all doors were secure.

When officials asked him to step behind the fence, he did so as he watched the propellers spin, first slowly in one direction, and then with increasing speed in the other. He listened to the finely tuned whine of the engine as he watched the pilot and copilot run through a checklist, their bowed heads visible through the front windows of the cockpit.

He put his hands on the fence as if to steady himself as he scanned the windows looking for Sal, but Sal was seated on the far side of the plane, so he waited until it had taxied down the runway, turned around, and began to accelerate before raising his right hand in a hearty wave as it sped by.

Had she seen him? Was he in her consciousness as intensely as she was in his? Would she find the answers she was seeking in Rhinebeck this time, or was this the beginning of a new nightmare in a life that had already known more than its share of strife?

When he reached into his pocket for his truck keys, he felt the feather in his fingers and knew that the path would not be clear. But if the feather could protect him as well as it had served Mara, then surely he would be able to deal with it, whatever *it* might turn out to be.

Chapter Nineteen
More Reflections

J oe Michael drove to the scrap yard next to the dock that he and Sal had rented to sort tsunami debris. A brisk wind was blowing in off the water and the stream of low white clouds along the mountains foretold a coming storm. For the moment, though, the warmth of the sun kept the chill from his bones as he walked among the piles of jetsam in the yard. The beach-lander had gone out this morning, so the yard was quiet, with all the sorting necessary having been done last week.

He stopped alongside a pile of rubber fishing floats. The faded shades of orange and yellow of the markers made the heap look like an artistic array. Missing were the stacks of crab pots and ropes so typical of Alaska fishing villages. Instead, there were piles of driftwood, and scraps of painted lumber and boards from houses and other buildings torn loose by the earthquake and tsunami in faraway Japan.

Occasional pieces of furniture, their once fine finishes since bleached and faded by their trip across the Pacific Ocean, were heaped in one corner—their value questionable, and kept only out of respect for the enormous loss to the people of that nation. Maybe one day there'd be a bonfire with a ceremony or something to dispose of them respectfully.

The scrap yard felt comforting, as if a tangible mirror of his own tumultuous past. Here among the battered, weathered, neatly sorted remnants of an entire nation, walked a battered, weathered Native elder, whose now orderly life gave little hint to all that had gone before.

Joe let his fingers search out the feather in his pocket, feeling the softness of its edges and gently twirling its spine lazily in the tips of his fingers. As he did so, his mind drifted, as a mental newsreel of his life played in his head.

He had been born not far from this very spot in a small cabin built of spruce logs hand scribed by his father and his uncle, and since lost to a wildfire several years ago.

He had been the oldest of two brothers and a sister who died of influenza before she was two. Stu, whose carelessness had caused the fire that cost Joe his first wife, had died still estranged from his brother a little over a year ago, leaving him with no family except for a smattering of cousins who still lived around Southeast. Of course, there was Della, Stu's only child, and he considered Mara and Doug family—but beyond that, except for Sal there was no one.

Even after the embezzlement and implications of wrongdoing that Stu had wrought on him, Joe had attended the memorial to his brother. He had done it for Della, he supposed. After all, Della was an innocent and her mother was the twin sister of Joe's beloved late wife. It had been right that he had been there for Della, and it had brought a modicum of closure for himself after he'd learned that Stu had never intended to harm him with the bank scheme, but had been simply a dying man trying to take care of the daughter he had abandoned at birth.

Joe sat on a log bench along an old shed at the edge of the yard. He leaned back on the metal siding now warmed by the sun and closed his eyes. He had learned to savor the sun in this place where it rained 360 or so days a year. He lifted his head with his face pointing towards the sky so as to capture every comforting ray. He might have fallen asleep; at least it seemed so when the low swoop of a passing magpie startled him into the present.

A board, lifted by a sudden gust of wind, dropped from the top of a pile onto the ground. He ducked reflexively, just as he had done countless times at the sound of gunfire in Vietnam.

He turned the collar of his jacket upward as fast-moving clouds obstructed the sun. How strange, to have been alone here for so long. It had felt peaceful, as though being near his roots had brought him home. The yard was seldom this quiet. He nodded heavenward in appreciation.

Sal had left him a refrigerator full of meals. He knew that in advance without having to look. Maybe he'd swing by to see Doug and Mara on the way home, and tomorrow, well tomorrow he might just decide to have coffee with Della. Then he'd go home and nap from around three until Sal called as usual at five—just to make sure he was okay and that he was eating the food that had "danged well better get ate or else . . ."

He smiled at the realness the sound of her voice had in his mind. Rhinebeck had better be good to Sal Kindle. It just had better darned well be good to her.

Chapter Twenty
Surprise Departure

T he next morning, Joe went back to the scrap yard. This time he climbed onto the old Cat D9 that he had picked up at auction a few years ago, and began moving some of the scrap metal that had become a minimountain in the center of the yard, pushing it over to the side of the lot that he had cleared of brush last week.

He had considered renting a compactor to crush it and bale it for salvage, but instead had decided to load it back onto the landing craft towards fall, and haul it over to Juneau for compacting once he had accumulated a few more piles. The recycling would cost him a pretty penny, but he had already received several generous offers for the final product that had assured him the effort would be worth the trouble.

After hopping down from the D9, he walked around the yard to check his work. Satisfied, he backed the machine close to the shoreline, and parked it well above the high-tide line.

On is way back to town, he stopped to check the salmon that he and Sal had hung in the old tradition for drying, satisfied that all was well there. Then he drove down onto the beach and threw some fish scraps out for the eagles. No one had ever complained at his tending to the birds that were the mascot for his old army unit, the "screaming eagles" of the 101st Airborne. As a matter of fact, most people really seemed to enjoy watching the majestic birds feed.

He loved to watch the eagles. Although there was plenty of salmon to keep them fat, they never turned down Joe's gift of a meal, and he never missed an opportunity to treat them.

He sat there until the incoming tide started lapping against his tires and another truck had pulled up alongside to launch a dinghy. With a polite nod to the other driver, a stranger and probably one of the summer residents, he let his dualie pull slowly up the beach to the shore and then drove aimlessly back into town, slowing regularly to check out things in general along the way.

He nearly got sideswiped when a fully equipped deluxe jeep came peeling by at a high rate of speed, causing a cloud of dust to obliterate his vision enough to force him to a full halt. Although it was not uncommon to have to dodge speeding four-wheelers on this road, generally local residents were respectful of each other and didn't engage in antics such as the one that had just occurred.

The incident irritated him more than usual. The last few weeks had shaken his resolve to never let life overpower him again. Almost without thinking, he reached for his gun, but instead felt his fingers touch the feather. It had come back to him for a reason and not knowing that reason was making him insecure—if insecure was the right word for a man as strong and steady as he.

Beside the feather and the gun, he felt the lifetime ferry pass he had placed there the other day.

It wasn't like him to have reached so easily for his gun. When he got home, he locked it in his gun safe for now. No sense carrying it when he felt this on edge. Then he packed a duffel bag, drove back down the same road he had come from, made a hard right turn into the ferry terminal, got out, locked his doors, and went inside.

By the time the ferry departed at noon, Joe was standing on the deck watching Hoonah fade from sight. He left a message on his phone before they moved out of cell phone range: *Gone for a week or so. I'm fine. Just needed some time. Keep an eye on the salmon I got hanging.* Then he turned the phone off, shoved it deep into his bag and stuffed the bag into the far corner of the bottom bunk of his stateroom.

Chapter Twenty-One
Home Again?

J oe Michael shuffled along the deck of the *Malaspina* following the invisible well-worn path left from his years of riding the Alaska State ferry. A deck worker nodded in recognition, but as he had always done before, the old man stared at his feet as he shuffled along.

A school of Dall's porpoises chased the wake of the ferry, causing him to smile ever so slightly at the sight. Effortless swimmers, so graceful and so swift—they were freedom, happiness, untethered spirits of the earth. Like the birds that soared above, they were unhampered by physical constraints. Perhaps he would return to earth as one of them one day after he had long left his human form. Did he really believe in such things? He felt the feather in his pocket and imagined that he did.

Once back in his stateroom, he checked his phone for messages. There were two from Mara; nothing from Sal. Mara would be worried. He should probably call her soon. Maybe he would, but not right now. He rubbed his tired eyes and put the phone away, hung his jacket over the end of a chair, readied for bed, then quickly fell into a sound sleep.

When the ferry docked in Juneau, he resisted the temptation to get off. Later, in Sitka, he used the five-hour layover to walk past the memorial to his family, who had perished in the fire accidentally started by Stu.

The brass memorial was tarnished a crusty blue by the sea air, but it seemed fitting that it so blended in with its surroundings. He paused to read the names of his family, saying each of them out loud in his soft, monotonic accent. He dabbed a tear from his eye as he choked back thoughts of wishing he were with them in heaven. But he wasn't with them in heaven; he had been left on this earth for some reason he still could not understand.

Was it Sal? Maybe he had been spared to take care of Sal? Or perhaps Mara or Della—maybe all of them? Whatever the case, his family was gone and he was not, so he wiped a sleeve gently across the brass plate and shuffled off down the street, speeding up slightly when he heard the blast of the ferry horn, before catching a cab to the ferry terminal some twelve miles out of town.

Once back on board the *Malaspina*, he stood on the deck watching Sitka fade away, before having dinner alone in a corner of the dining room and then heading to his stateroom for the night. He slept through stops in Wrangell, Petersburg, Ketchikan, and most of the trip south to Bellingham. Then, once he was back on land, he did the unexpected and got on a plane to Rhinebeck, New York.

Chapter Twenty-Two
Destined Path?

After renting a motel room near the airport some fifty miles or so from Rhinebeck, and still not sure why he had decided to come to New York, Joe dialed his wife's phone only to get a voicemail saying that she would return the call later.

When morning came too soon, he had a leisurely breakfast before checking his voicemail to hear Sal calling and wondering why he wasn't answering. Her message said that she had talked to Mara, who had told her about his need to be away for a few days.

"I'm fine, Sal. I'll call later," was the message he left in return when he again got only the voicemail on her phone.

He rented a car and set out for Rhinebeck, enjoying the drive along the Hudson River Valley filled with its grand estates, parks, and golf courses.

The area was nothing like Alaska and nothing like he had seen before. There was a quietness and a civility to the landscape that though developed, had been done so in the days long before Alaska had first enjoyed statehood, and long after his Native American brothers had inhabited the area.

He hadn't brought any special clothes for the trip, but his casual neatness made him blend in as just another tourist, although at some point he wisely chose to lose the ball cap that he had been sporting since his years of travel on the ferry.

Once in Rhinebeck, he passed several of the old violet houses that Sal had spoken about, and even passed the old LaMonte estate, marked by a small metal sign nailed to the stone fence surrounding it.

He almost pulled in to inquire about Sal, but decided not to, again trying to reach her on her phone. This time she answered.

"Joey? That finally you?" she bellowed, after first answering in the perfect diction of her upbringing. "Mara said ya took off on the ferry again cuz ya was upset. What's that, Joey."

They spotted each other at the same time as he rounded a corner near one of the violet houses. He saw Sal's mouth drop open as she pressed the *off* button on her phone and made her way to the car.

"Joe," she said simply, using proper English and a refined tone of voice.

"Yup. It's me," Joe answered.

"But, what are you doing here? I mean . . . Joe, you came all the way from Hoonah?"

"Well, you did," he replied, "and so I figured you might need me. I figured you might like some help. I figured I might like to see this place. I figured you missed me."

"No one knows about you here," Sal answered, stepping back from embracing her husband.

The move took him by surprise.

"I'm sorry if I'm intruding," he said softly. "I thought you'd be happy."

"I am happy, Joey," Sal answered, stepping forward to embrace him. "I don't know what's wrong with me for acting this way. This whole thing—this whole experience about returning here—has been unsettling and put me off balance."

"I can see that it has, Sal," Joe said.

Rattled by her unexpected coolness, he walked away from her along a worn path that surrounded the violet house, while Sylvia LaMonte stood silently watching. Minutes later, he came back up the other side of the old greenhouse and faced her.

"I'm staying at the Best Western near Hyde Park," he told her. "You can find me there if you need me."

He didn't wait for her to answer. Climbing into the rental car, he backed up slowly and retraced his path out of town, never looking back—not even in the rearview mirror—as he left.

Perhaps coming to Rhinebeck had been a bad idea. Then again, maybe it was time for the truth about his and Sal/Sylvia's relationship to come out. Either way it would survive this latest set of occurrences in her life, or it wouldn't. He took the feather from his pocket and held it up to the light. The red dot shone, caught by the rays of the sun.

Was Sal the reason he had it now? Was his very life's path with Sal in the crosshairs of destiny? Her actions told him it could be. He placed the feather carefully back in his pocket and kept driving. The serenity of the valley now felt more like a façade covering the endless truths of this region's storied past. This historical place, where people who had walked here long before he and Sal had faced their own tests and trials, made him feel somehow insignificant—small, in that way of powerlessness; powerless, in that way of his life being just another speck on the current mantle of this region.

Maybe he should never have come here, but deep inside, he knew life was unfurling as it was supposed to, although not necessarily as he wished it would.

Chapter Twenty-Three
Promise to Come Home

Sylvia LaMonte Kindle Michael found the Best Western Hotel near Hyde Park, arriving just in time to see her husband locking up the rental car to go inside.

Joe Michael looked up when he saw her, a slight upturn of one side of his mouth his only expression.

"Sal? Or is it Sylvia that I should call you now?" he said dryly.

"I loved ya the minute I seen ya fer the first time and I love ya now, Joey," Sal said, sounding like the Alaskan woman he had married.

She threw her arms around Joe Michael's chest and squeezed him so hard that he finally had to push her away, just so he could breathe.

"It's been hard, Sal," he told her. "Hard in many ways."

Sal nodded.

"I never thought I'd care for another woman after I lost my family to that fire. Then, when I met you, you almost seemed to be too much woman for an old guy like me."

Sal's eyes softened as a slow smile moved across her lips.

"I was proud when you said you'd marry me, and I'm still proud to call you my wife, but if you—if things have changed—if you need to get away from what we have going, well—"

Joe took several deep breaths, closing his eyes as if to capture his thoughts before continuing.

"I can see how beautifully you fit in here," he said. "And I could never fit in here—although I'd try if you asked me to. I would, Sal. I'd try."

He watched tears well up in the eyes of the woman he had always thought of as tough as nails and too stubborn to bend to common human emotion.

"I'm ashamed of the way I was back there today," Sal said, once again reverting to her base dialect. "It's like this place does something to a person—takes over their spirit and keeps them from connecting with who they are inside."

She looked up at Joe Michael, her eyes pleading for understanding. He looked deep within them in return, his puzzled expression revealing the uncertainty of not fully knowing this woman to whom he was married.

Was this why he had come here—to learn the truth? To see with his own eyes what his mind could not grasp?

"I can't tell you that I understand when I don't," Joe Michael said.

He reached into his pocket, touching the feather, secure at its reassuring presence.

"I wouldn't be here if I didn't love you," he told her. "There's no question about my love for you and there's no doubt in my mind about your love for me—but as Sal, my wife. It's the fact that you are not just my Sal that—"

"I'm not going to try to force you to stay, Joey," Sylvia said softly. "It's not my place to help you decide. All that's important to me is standing right here in front of me. The rest of it—well the rest of it threatens to destroy me just like it destroyed my Bert. If you choose to stay, I'll be stronger for it, but if you can't stay, then just know that I'll return to Hoonah as soon as I've straightened out what should have been straightened out long ago. Then, I'll be home, Joey. I promise you I will come home."

Chapter Twenty-Four
Oh! Deer!

Sal walked beside her husband into the Best Western and joined him for dinner in the motel dining room before retiring with him to his room for the night. It had been a long time since they had been truly alone.

Sleep came easily when it arrived, but not before they had spent all the time they needed savoring each other's nearness. This time there was no pretense, there were no daily rituals to perform, and there was no worry about phone calls. There was no need for vigilance in case someone decided to drop in. There was just the two of them and the solace of their aloneness in the night.

Joe held her tightly and she let him. This was love. This was safety from the world—he her protector from all things outside themselves, and she his.

Morning came too soon and while Sal dressed, she told her husband about the dinner scheduled for this coming Saturday at the local golf club. Some of her old friends were planning a big welcome after having learned of her return to Rhinebeck. It would be an elaborate affair of feigned casualness so common to the area—one in which suggested sporting attire would serve as the barometer of the commonness so many wished they possessed, but were ill equipped to understand.

"Please come with me. It's time for them to meet my husband," she said.

He agreed, although reluctantly. But for her he would go in spite of his obvious discomfort at being in this strange place. Her smile told him he was doing the right thing.

"We'd better go shopping for some casual clothes," she told him.

"What's wrong with these?" he asked, pointing to the nylon bomber jacket and canvas pants that were his usual attire.

"Nothing," Sal answered. "Nothing except they are not contrived enough to blend in here."

She laughed lightly at the use of the word *contrived*. Hadn't she, the Alaska wilderness woman, become the snob. But what other word was there to describe the reality that only certain carefully thought-out images of *casual* would work for these folks, whose image and persona had been watchfully crafted since birth?

Joe squinted but didn't argue. Sal knew what she was doing so he might as well just go along. He would dress to please her and he would do his best to complement her in this place so foreign to his soul. After all, hadn't she done the same for him in their life up in Alaska?

They settled on a white linen, long-sleeved shirt for Joe and a pair of light colored slacks that had a perfect crease down the front. Sal also steered him towards a pair of soft Italian leather loafers, while choosing a long floral print dress in shades of light blue, over which she wore a matching cardigan sweater. A long lavender silk scarf wrapped loosely around her neck and a pair of taupe-colored flat ballet shoes completed her look.

"I thought I'd drive down to see the Vietnam Veterans' wall while I'm here," Joe told her, once their shopping was done. "The dinner's several days away. I'll be back in time."

"I know you will, Joey," she said. "Just meet me at the club at seven on Saturday. "I've already left word that the doorman should let you straight in and have someone bring you to my table."

"Are you sure about this, Sal? Sure you want to be seen with me?" Joe said with such a straight face that it made her laugh.

"Ya kiddin' me, Joey! Not just sure, but proud to call a hunk a man like you ma man," Sal laughed, sounding like her old self again.

"I love you, Sal," Joe Michael said with uncharacteristic forthrightness.

"I love you too, Joe," she answered.

~ ~ ~

Sylvia watched her husband walk back to his motel room through the rear-view mirror of her own car as she slowly exited the parking lot of the motel. Once out of sight of the man she loved more than any other she had ever known, a glance in that same mirror showed that the furrowed brow and downturned lips of worry had replaced her smile.

She scrunched her left shoulder trying to loosen the tightness that was rapidly spreading up her neck, but nothing she did brought relief from the tension-induced cramping.

Life had been so perfect until Elzianne had shown up in Hoonah. Now the very essence of her content, her wonderful life with Joe Michael, was in jeopardy. If not for Elzianne bringing up the past, she and Joe would likely have finished out their lives without him ever learning of her past—a past that would not disappear, no matter how hard she tried to erase it.

It wasn't in the way of deceit that she had kept it from him, but more in the way of having moved on to a life free from the constraints it had bound her with. He, of course, knew she was from New York, and he also knew that she had been married to Bert Kindle, and that Bert had met an untimely death. But the details of her privileged upbringing had remained with the past in a place that Sylvia LaMonte had been sure would remain eternally unnecessary to visit.

She had just about decided to pull over to work the knot out of her shoulder when a deer ran out from a thicket of brush alongside the road. When she swerved, the deer suddenly leaped over her car and ran uninjured off into a field.

Joe Michael was already halfway to Washington DC when someone found Sal's car in the ditch. How long had she been lying there? Her watch said it was 6 p.m. The last time she had looked, it had been ten that morning.

"I'm fine. I'm fine," she insisted, finally agreeing to let the rescuer drive her to the hospital for an exam after he pointed out that the blood on her face was dried, and telling her that she must have been there for some time. And, but for the goose egg on her forehead, she was fine as far as she or the doctors could tell, so by 10 p.m. she was back in her hotel room getting ready for sleep.

When her phone rang as she was getting her nightclothes on, Sylvia LaMonte saw that the caller ID said *Williams, Mara*. She stared at it quizzically, then deleted the call, not bothering to check the message. She repeated the sequence the next three times the phone rang showing the same caller ID. A fourth call was from a *Michael, J* and she deleted that one, too, before turning the pesky thing off for the night.

What was it with all these calls anyway? She put the phone in the back corner of her drawer so it wouldn't bother her and went to bed.

Chapter Twenty-Five
The Wall

J oe Michael's trip to Washington D.C. was uneventful considering that he was an Alaska Native who had never been this far east. Perhaps his navigation of the busy freeways had been helped by the GPS on his rental car. A person didn't need such devices in Alaska, where the ocean and mountains formed directional guides, and where the road system was so simple that it was almost impossible to get lost.

Whatever the case, he had gotten there without many wrong turns, checked into a motel near the nation's capitol, and visited as many landmarks as he could work in before stopping at the Vietnam Wall of Honor on the last day there.

The monument, striking in its simplicity, served as a backdrop to the hundreds of people who were slowly moving past it. He couldn't help but notice the contrast of life against the long, black, banner that held the names of 58,000 who had died in the service of their country. If the artist had foreseen this eventuality—the way that life had sprung from death—then she had indeed been wise beyond her years.

He started in the middle. He wasn't sure why. Who among all these names did he know? A name popped into his consciousness. He searched for it, and it was there. Then he did the same for two more, before raw emotion overcame him and tears began to trickle down his cheeks.

He wiped them away. Crying wouldn't bring them back. Thank God it wasn't his name up there, although it easily could have been. He began to tremble inside. Why had he been spared? Was the life he had led even as worthy as the lives of those lost might have been?

A woman brushed past him and touched a name on the wall. Who was she? Sister? Wife? Daughter? Stranger? A small child clung to her coat hem. Was that her grandfather's name on the wall?

Suddenly he had to sit down. The wall was no longer a cold piece of granite holding an endless stream of the names of strangers. The wall was a living tribute to all who had given their lives in that war. These visitors were the roots it had sprung as it grasped towards life—expanding, embracing, broadening the consciousness of all who had come searching for each lone name of someone who had served his or her country with honor.

He put his head into his hands. Why couldn't they have lived? Why had each of them had to die? Why had he been spared? Had he lived his life well enough to deserve to have escaped that wall?

He reflected on is own recent strife. It felt like nothing. At least he had lived. What could the lives of each of these soldiers have become? He held back from touching the names, as though touching them would pull him with them into the wall. Instead he bought a book of all the names from a vendor near the memorial. He might read each and every one of them—or not. But what he would do was hold them near his heart and within the safety of his own home. He could protect them there and shelter them from the countless eyes that wept at their sight.

He didn't look back as he left. He couldn't look back. If he did, he would lie there with them and never get up again.

Chapter Twenty-Six
Who's Chair?

It seemed like everyone from Rhinebeck was at the dinner Saturday. Sylvia LaMonte greeted them one by one as the guests arrived. Yes, of course she had missed them all—or so her words declared.

"Do say," she replied, when someone mentioned that Elzianne was up in Alaska on a buying trip. "I've been wondering what she's been up to."

"It *is* so sad that the violet houses have fallen into disrepair."

"Yes, an effort to set up a foundation to restore them would be a worthy project."

She glanced at the empty chair beside her as guests seated themselves for dinner.

Where in the world was her husband?

She looked at her watch, trying hard not to show her uneasiness. She had just brushed a wrinkle out of her skirt when the maitre d' arrived at her table and pulled out a chair for an elderly man who was wearing a white linen shirt and finely creased trousers.

"I'm sorry," she said, leaning back to speak to the maitre d', "but this place is reserved for my husband."

Joe Michael stepped back.

"But, Ms. LaMonte, this gentleman assures me that he is your husband."

"Well sir, I can assure you that although this person cuts as fine a figure as any girl could hope to attract, Mr. Bert Kindle is a good four inches taller and about twenty pounds lighter than this gentleman, so if you will be so kind as to escort him from our table, I will reserve this chair for the man it actually belongs to."

"But, Ms. LaMonte . . ." the maitre d' began.

Joe Michael did not wait for any further exchange. He had looked directly into the eyes of his wife and had seen no sign of recognition in them. The large bruise on her forehead troubled him, but she seemed otherwise fine and he would not make a scene.

Had Sal fooled him again? What was going on here? Was he losing his mind? Was she? The night in the motel had been wonderful, cementing their love forever—or so he had thought—but this was unexpected.

He took several deep breaths, imagining that the space around his heart was open and free instead of tight and choking like it really felt.

He couldn't have misread her the other night. The love they shared had been real. This was not real. He turned around and moved towards her.

"Sal? What's going on?"

Her smile was as genuine as it was genteel.

"I'm so sorry to embarrass you, sir. You seem like a kind man, but I really must insist that you acknowledge that you are mistakenly here even after I have clearly told you that this place is reserved for my husband, Bert Kindle."

The maitre d' stepped back, taking Joe Michael by the arm and whispering into his ear.

"I believe you are who you say you are, sir, because it is common knowledge in Rhinebeck that Bert Kindle has been dead for several years. However, for the sake of decorum, please allow me to escort you outside so as to avert any further disruption."

Joe Michael went willingly. At the door, he showed the maitre d' his ID, including the picture of him and Sal that he had carried since their wedding day.

"Yes, it does appear to be Ms. LaMonte in this photo obviously taken during some type of travel adventure, sir, but this is not a matter I can allow myself to become involved in. I am simply the maitre d'. I do plead for your understanding."

"She had a bump on her head . . ." Joe Michael said.

"Although it's really not my place to say, sir, it is common knowledge that there was a minor accident, but that the hospital checked and released Ms. LaMonte," the maitre d' replied.

Joe Michael simply nodded before walking out the door and back to his car. He had pledged to stand behind his wife no matter what was coming down. He reached for the feather in his pocket. At least it was still there. Maybe he would wait here and talk to Sal after dinner. No. There would be too many people around. Maybe he would wait for her at her hotel. No. That seemed too confrontational. Maybe he would just disappear—get back on the ferry and cruise Alaska like he had for the years before meeting Sal. No. That had lost its appeal. He was older now. Ready for a more stable life. He laughed quietly. Stable life. What did he know of a stable life?

On the drive back to Hyde Park he made his decision. Tomorrow he would return to Alaska. He needed to think. Then he would decide what to do.

Chapter Twenty-Seven
Déjà vu?

Two days after boarding the ferry in Bellingham, Joe Michael again shuffled along the deck of the *Malaspina*, this time more lost and more deflated than ever before. Gone were the fancy new rimless glasses that Sal had chosen for him. In their place was the comfortable black-rimmed pair that he had worn for more years than he had been married to the second love of his life. Gone, too, was the thin gold band he had worn on the ring finger of his left hand since the two of them had vowed to be together until death.

Perhaps he had been a fool to think that he could find love again, especially now that he was in his 70s. Or maybe it had been wishful thinking that had prompted him to think that a woman as feisty and adventurous as Sal Kindle had walked into his life devoid of any hidden truths about her past.

Whatever the case, even though his heart had not let go of the love he felt for her, his mind had told him that he must try, and so he had shed the ring and the glasses as the two most powerful reminders that he and Sal had ever walked hand in hand through life. Instead, he wandered the decks of the ferry just as he had done after losing his first wife to the horrible house fire that had taken his entire family.

He had left Rhinebeck without trying to see her again. What would have been the point? She obviously either didn't know him or was playing some kind of game with his heart, and she had "people" looking out for her—lots and lots of people. Whatever the case, it had all left him confused and so he had run away, just as he had done after losing his first wife, only this time, he couldn't quite put his finger on the reason why.

If he and Sal were meant to be together again, he reasoned, she would find him or he would find her or they would find each other. Whatever the case, suddenly he had been thrust into some kind of survival mode and unable to do any more than retreat into the safety of his own self, and that was a familiar place even though littered with the shallow graves that held his memories of Vietnam.

A humpback whale breached so close to the ferry that the huge vessel leaned slightly in the water under the weight of passengers trying to get a glimpse should it surface again. He pushed open the door to the main entryway that held the purser's office and the stairways to the upper and lower decks. Then he made his way across the width of the ferry and pushed open the door to the deck on the other side.

No one was there. He looked heavenward, silently asking for the whale to breach again so as to keep the passengers away from him on the other side.

He stared down into the clear green water. Several jellyfish bobbed just below the surface, their tentacles seeming to reach over ten—maybe twenty—feet in length, straight downward into the water. He gripped the deck rail, as if to steel himself from the impulse to join them. Then he slowly made his way back to his stateroom and had dinner brought to his room.

When the ferry stopped in Sitka the next day, he would stay there for a few days, visit the memorial to his family, and maybe take a walk through Totem Park. He knew a couple of carvers there. Carvers were good storytellers. They respected tradition and all the deep meanings of life. He might ask if he could carve for a while himself. That would require special conditions, but maybe he could carve like he had done when he was a younger man. Carving had always brought him peace.

He again felt the feather against the fingers he had shoved inside his pocket. It gave him comfort and a sense that rightness would prevail.

After hanging his jacket over the end of a chair, he readied for bed and slept soundly.

Tomorrow Sitka might bring him the answers, perhaps solace. It had been so once before, and perhaps it would be so now.

Chapter Twenty-Eight
Roots

The next day in Sitka, Joe found the son of his friend, John, beginning a new pole outside the carving pavilion in Totem Park.

"You are John's son," he said when he arrived.

A slight nod in response told him that he was right.

Joe sat down on a log bench and watched as John's son began to carve. Within the hour, John himself arrived and sat next to Joe on the bench. The two men remained silent as John's son began to carve, with John often getting up to supervise some fine point about the carving.

By day's end, the first two feet of the totem had been roughed out, having met the approval of the elder carver, who told his son they would continue tomorrow.

For the next several days, Joe Michael returned to Totem Park to watch John and his son work. On the fourth day, John got up as usual, but this time took the carving tools from his son and handed them to Joe, directing him to carve the place five feet from the designated bottom of the currently side-lying pole, in a place that would be directly in line with the top of Joe's shoulders once the pole was erected.

Joe Michael began his work, carving a feather in the shape of a crescent moon against the backdrop of the sun. For an entire day he carved, before returning the tools to John, who nodded in quiet understanding.

"You will return for the Potlatch next year," he told him. "And you will help to burn the end of the pole and help us erect it."

Joe Michael nodded and embraced his friend before turning and walking away.

He would return next year and he would keep living so that he could. His friend, John, had found a way to make sure that he would.

Chapter Twenty-Nine
A Good Cessna 206

The flight back to Juneau was fast and a respite of sorts for the tired and worn Joe Michael. He had made so many friends on the ferry system over the years, that privacy would have been impossible during this time when he simply needed time to think, so he bought a plane ticket back to Hoonah.

Several times he caught himself reminiscing about flying his own Piper Super Cub wherever he wanted to go. He had spent countless hours flying over Alaska, having outfitted the plane with a prop that would let him fly "low and slow" as he liked to call it. He missed flying, but his heart condition had put an end to that particular activity and so now he flew on a commercial junket, still feeling the surge of adrenaline that had always made him love to fly.

He really didn't like flying on commercial flights. All the rules and restrictions stifled him and made him feel like a nameless entity among so many other nameless entities in the sky. There weren't any options for flying out of Hoonah on a private plane. Lots of people had them, but no one that he felt he could ask to take him on a flight all the way to New York.

He could probably ask Ben Edwards to help him out if this thing in Rhinebeck was going to require any more trips back and forth. But Ben was about to become a father again, so even though he knew full well that Ben would bend over backwards to help him, it was an option that he just would not pursue—if, that is, if he were to go back there again. Strange, how thoughts of Rhinebeck and Sal kept popping into his brain when he had tried so hard to shut out thoughts of the path their life had taken.

Maybe recertifying his status as a pilot could be an option. He could buy a new plane. He'd seen one for sale in Juneau right before he left. Maybe he'd look into it. Maybe he was being foolish. No doctor was going to sign off on a flight physical for an elderly man with a heart condition. He took a deep breath and let out an audible sigh.

"Yes, I'm okay," he told the passenger sitting next to him. "I was just thinking hard."

It had to be some kind of serendipity then, when he saw a red and white Cessna 206 sitting in front of Beachmoppers when he walked over in the morning after having arrived in Hoonah the night before.

The morning was sunny, showing promise of being one of those rare days when no rain fell in Hoonah. The plane shone in the sun, looking like it had been waxed to a high polish.

Every part was polished to perfection, including the high-speed propeller, which was obviously new. A set of matching floats sat in the yard telling him that someone was definitely in the process of getting the aircraft ready for use.

"She's a beauty, isn't she Joe?" Doug Williams said as he joined Joe Michael in the yard.

"Yes. A beauty," Joe Michael answered. "It's no Super Cub, but it's still a beauty."

"I couldn't have asked for a better deal," Doug said, answering Joe Michael's silent question about who the plane belonged to.

"Is it the one from Juneau?" Joe Michael asked, recognizing the color as being the same as the one he had seen.

"It is. How did you know about it?" Doug answered.

"Saw it there recently," Joe answered, "on my way south."

"We've been worried about you, Joe," Doug said. "Mara's been frantic. Luckily the shop's been busy, so the time's gone by quickly."

"Didn't mean to make you worry," Joe answered.

"Where's Sal?" Doug asked.

"Rhinebeck. Rhinebeck, New York," Joe answered.

"Joe!" Mara exclaimed, rushing to greet him. "We've been worried sick."

"Didn't mean to make you worry," Joe repeated. "But I see you managed to keep busy picking out a Cessna."

Joe Michael ran his hand along the fuselage as he walked absently around the plane.

"Where's Sal?" Mara said, following him.

"Like I told Doug, Rhinebeck. Sal's in Rhinebeck, New York."

"When's she coming back?" Mara asked.

Joe kept examining the plane and didn't answer.

"She's all right, isn't she? Joe? Is Sal all right? She is coming back, isn't she?"

Joe turned around and looked directly into her eyes.

"Got any water on for tea?" he asked. "Some hot tea would be real nice."

Chapter Thirty
Unarmed Robbery

Both Doug and Mara sat transfixed as Joe Michael described his visit to Rhinebeck.

"This explains a lot," Mara said. "No wonder Sal's been so distracted."

"You said she had a bump on her head," Doug said. "Could that explain her behavior on that last night?"

Joe Michael got up and carried his cup to the sink. Then he walked over and put a gentle hand on Mara's shoulder before walking out the door.

"He acts like he's giving up," Mara said. "It's like the life has been sucked out of him."

"He's been through a lot, for sure," Doug answered, "but Sal is his life and we just can't let him give up on her no matter how helpless he feels."

For the rest of the day, the two busied themselves with bringing new stock into Beachmoppers. Tomorrow a cruise ship was due in, so they needed to be ready.

It was the second hot, sunny day in a row and everyone in Hoonah, it seemed, was in a great mood. Gardens were being cultivated, houses were being painted, people were walking everywhere, and fishing was in full swing.

"I saw Elzianne and her entourage walking by yesterday," Mara called to Doug, as she stepped outside to check on Thor.

The dog bounded up to her, jumping up to lick her face. Laughing at his exuberance, she pushed him down and reached for the blue bowl to get him some fresh water. Thor jumped up again. Even he felt playful in the summer sun, but Mara pushed him down and told him to sit/stay for emphasis.

Where was the bowl? Had he knocked it under a bush or something? She hoped he hadn't broken it.

She stopped to admire the petunias that were trailing beautifully from the five-gallon bucket she had planted them in, and then stooped to pull up some chickweed that had taken too strong of a hold and needed to go. She shifted the park bench a few inches to level it, reached under a few bushes, but still no sign of the bowl.

"Doug! Have you seen Thor's bowl?"

When he didn't answer, she went inside to ask him again, but he wasn't there, so she looked around the sink area and saw that the bowl was not there either.

Just then Della came in.

"Della, have you seen Thor's bowl?"

"It was there yesterday," Della said. "I remember that because I put fresh water in it for Thor."

"Well it's gone now," Mara said.

"Maybe someone took it," Della said.

Mara gave her a look.

"Della!"

Della brushed past her, unconcerned.

"There's probably something else we can put his water in," she said.

"Okay, Della. Just keep your eyes open for it, okay. I kind of liked that bowl. Maybe it'll turn up."

Mara found an old dog dish and put fresh water out for Thor. Then she went in to fix herself some lunch, flipping on the TV as she did. It was then that she saw the "breaking news" headline flash across the screen.

PRICELESS JAPANESE EDO PERIOD PORCELAIN FLOWER BOWL
FOUND ON REMOTE ALASKA ISLAND.

There on the screen, stood Elzianne LaMonte holding Thor's water bowl. She turned up the sound just in time to hear Elzianne speak.

"The New York Cultural Museum is pleased to announce the acquisition of this rare Edo Period flower bowl, where it was discovered near remote Hoonah, Alaska. Fortunately, members of our expedition were able to recover it from its precarious location at the feet of one of the area's wild dogs. Unlike the typical green glaze used on porcelains of this period, this bowl is one of only two known to exist in the color of robin's egg blue and its value is presumed to be priceless. It will be place on indefinite display at the museum beginning next week."

Mara muted the sound. Unbelievable! Not only had Elzianne obviously stolen the bowl, but she was brazen enough to go on national TV to not only distort the truth, but to brag about it.

"There's no way you're going to be able to prove it was your bowl," Doug told her later.

"Well, it was my bowl," Mara sputtered.

"You got hundreds of dollars for a lawyer to try to prove it?" he asked.

Mara nodded and walked away. The fact was that even though Brad had left her comfortably well off, neither of them had the kind of money it would take to go up against Elzi LaMonte and her high-priced New York legal team.

"I can't even prove she was here that day," she told Doug later. "Della says she saw her here, but she didn't see her take the bowl."

"The woman is as evil as Sal said she is," Doug answered. "She's a special kind of evil."

Chapter Thirty-One
Photographic Proof

"We have proof that the bowl is ours," a law student named Dennis, who was working at Beachmoppers for the summer, commented when Mara told everyone what she had seen on TV.

"The bowl is listed right here along with a picture in our catalog of every piece of recovered debris. We also have the date it was recovered, pictures of the recovery, and the date it was brought to Hoonah," Dennis added. "Sal thought it was excessive—you know, all the documentation—but one of the archeology majors and I decided that it was easy enough to do, especially in this age of digital cameras. You never know—that was our thinking. Looks like our detail work might have paid off this time."

"But, still, how can we prove it was *our* bowl? They said there are two," Mara asked.

Dennis cocked his head and looked perplexed.

"I'm sorry," Mara said. "I just don't trust that woman and her high-powered attorneys."

"If I remember correctly, the bowl has a unique dip in the glaze on one side," Dennis said. "It caught my attention because it told me it must be handmade."

"Hmm," Mara answered.

"I remember taking extra photos of it because I liked the color. I thought it was unusual for its color. I don't know, there was something about it that made me notice it more than a lot of the stuff we've been pulling in. To tell you the truth, I was kind of surprised when you decided to use it for a dog dish."

Mara blushed. After sifting through so much debris, she had seen the bowl as just another artifact among thousands and thousands of others.

"I guess Thor was thirsty and I needed something for the water that day," she said simply. "Sal had no use for it and it was just too pretty to throw away."

"I'll look for the photos tonight," Dennis said. "I haven't gotten them all cataloged yet, so it might take me a day or two to go through them. I have over twenty thousand photos of tsunami debris already. I even had to take them off my hard drive to free up some space. It's because I shoot in RAW."

"RAW?" Mara asked.

"Raw format," Dennis answered. "It's the most perfect. It has the highest resolution. It captures everything. If I find it, and I *will* find it, we'll have all the proof we need that the bowl was ours."

Mara smiled at Dennis. What a great idea Doug had come up with in hiring the college students for Beachmoppers. At first Sal had wanted to hire locals, but when no one seemed interested, Doug had posted flyers on an Alaska tourism website with a worldwide distribution, that also posted other summer jobs for college students.

"It's about the adventure," Doug had told Mara. "And those are just the type of workers we want. Not everyone wants to work in the hospitality industry. I think we'll find our workers easily enough."

Doug had been right. Applications for jobs at Beachmoppers had far exceeded available openings even though Sal was paying slightly less than the major hotel and cruise lines were offering. He had been careful in interviewing them, too, choosing those most focused on the sciences and who displayed more than the usual attention to detail.

Dennis had almost not made the cut. His long ponytail, carefully manicured nails, and the double ear piercings on each ear had made Doug cringe. No guy wears that many hoops on his body, he had speculated, and if he does, he's probably too narcissistic to pay attention to all the clutter he was going to have to sift through for this job.

But Doug had been wrong. Dennis had proven to be not only a leader, but one of the most articulate of all the workers. It didn't hurt that the female crew members were constantly vying for his attention, and that the guys wanted to be just like him to look cool.

Now it looked like Dennis was going to prove his worth again. Doug gave him a friendly slap on his shoulder as he walked off after having arrived midway through his conversation with Mara.

"Let us know what we can do to help you out with this," he said. "If you need me to cover a shift for you or whatever—just let me know."

Dennis nodded. "I appreciate that, but I'm good. Just give me a day or two. I might need to borrow your printer, but that's about it, man—but thanks."

"I'm off to study for my flight exam," Doug told Mara. "If all goes as planned, I can test out next week and then we can start flying our new plane."

Thirty-Two
Morally, Ethically, Passionately Right

As Dennis had promised, he searched for and found several pictures of the blue bowl, including a couple that showed the unique dip in the glaze that he had referred to.

Not only had he found the right documentation, but he forwarded it—along with a detailed account of its theft and subsequent publication on TV—to his father, Dennis Connor, who was a senior partner in a large Boston law firm that coincidentally specialized in acquisitions and value assessments.

As Dennis had predicted, a copy of a letter sent to Elzianne LaMonte was sitting on the counter at KonaJanes by week's end. In the letter was the assertion that the bowl had washed ashore as tsunami debris, had been in the possession of Mara and Doug at Beachmoppers, and even included a picture of the "family pet" Thor drinking from the bowl.

Considering the case to be close to resolution—especially in view of a sternly worded admonition stating that further claims to the true ownership of the bowl would be met with vigorous pursuit of all available legal options—no one was more surprised than Dennis Connor Jr. when a lear jet carrying Dennis Connor Sr. landed in Hoonah the following week with two members of a legal team that vowed to take the case for having the bowl returned to its rightful owners all the way to the supreme court if necessary, just so that justice could prevail.

"The legal snakes representing Elzianne LaMonte have scraped the bottom of the barrel of tolerance and decency by their carelessly worded assertion that my son has photoshopped pictures of this bowl and this location to suit the needs of those she refers to as 'the opportunistic, publicity-seeking, avaricious townfolk,'" he said, thrusting a packet of papers in Mara's hands.

And if that were not complication enough in reclaiming the priceless bowl, he then presented Mara with a handwritten note from the minister of museum affairs in Honshu, Japan, that he had received just that morning, pleading for the return of the recently unearthed artifact to help preserve the deep history of the Japanese people.

"If you are sincere in your offer to assist us," Mara stated, "then surely we must allow you to pursue this—not just for ourselves, but for Sal Kindle, and Joe Michael, and simply for the sake of rightness and justice for all concerned."

Doug put his arm around his wife and kissed her on the forehead.

"Wow," Della said. "That was some speech, Mara."

"GrrWoof!" Thor added.

"I would not be here if I were not sincere, Ms. Williams," he said flatly. "Now, if you'll excuse me, I'd like to visit with my son for a few hours before returning to Boston in the morning. But before I leave, I will ask you to allow my team members to obtain as much information from you as they can."

"Well, Sal—the person who owns this business—is currently out of state, and her husband has been sadly shaken by that very turn of events," Mara tried to explain. "And both their and our own financial resources are limited against the unfettered capital available to someone like Elzianne LaMonte and, presumably, the museum in New York."

Dennis Connor Sr. waved his hand as if to dismiss all talk of charges before speaking again.

"But it was to you that she entrusted the bowl?"

"I guess so," Mara answered. "She said she didn't want it and didn't think it was worth anything and told me to do whatever I wanted to with it, so instead of throwing it away like she asked me to, I used it for Thor's water bowl."

"And you have witnesses to that conversation?" Dennis Connor Sr. asked.

"I heard it," Della spoke up.

"I did, too," Doug said.

"And, actually, Father, I guess I did too, as Ms. Kindle specifically told me that she didn't know why Mara insisted on keeping that old bowl around when it could get stepped on or broken and—let's see, how did she put it—yes, and 'get ma danged rear side sued fer injuries,' is what she said to me. I remember it because she had stopped me from photographing it one day saying that I was wasting time when there was important stuff to be cataloged."

"If we can build a strong enough case for ownership of this bowl—and I think we can—and if we can get it safely returned, then if I understand things correctly, you stand to make more money than any of us could ever hope to spend if you can find a suitable buyer," Dennis Connor Sr. said. "And should that occur, then a reimbursement for our travel time and expenses would be all that I would ask. On the other hand, returning it to its rightful owners—the people of Japan, would result in a complete waiving of all fees from our firm. The final decision on the disposition of the bowl once it is recovered will rest completely in your hands."

Mara smiled reassuredly at the half smile and wink that Mr. Connor had displayed during the discussion about potential costs.

"But first, we must pursue the proper channels, and in view of this recent reply to our initial letter, they are not going to willingly hand over such a valuable item without a fight."

"On behalf of my wife and Sal Kindle and her husband, Joe Michael, I would like to thank you for coming here and for personally taking this matter on," Doug said.

"Well, young man, there are only a few times in a man's life when he chooses to passionately pursue justice to this extent, and this time for me is one of them. I am happy to do this not only for you, but for the sake of my son's credibility, as an example to him of how justice must be sought, and for myself—simply because it is the right thing, and the moral thing, and the ethical thing to do."

Chapter Thirty-Three
A Little Solitude

M ara and Doug Williams walked hand in hand along the beach. The sunset was spectacular and the water unusually calm. Overhead, several eagles swooped for their evening meal before settling into the branches of the thick spruce stands that marked the area. Across the water, Graveyard Island stood silently beneath a thin layer of mist. In the distance, the dull roar of an ATV was the only sound except for the screeches of the gulls and the occasional high-pitched call of the eagles.

A few silver salmon splashed across the calmness as they jumped en route to their spawning grounds—their white bellies catching what was left of the sun. A slight rustle in the brush made Doug reach for his pistol, but it was only a loose dog and not a bear. He called Thor to his side anyway, before leading Mara down closer to the water, where they found a large rock that they could both sit on.

He knew she was thinking about the bowl just like he was. He also knew that the bowl and its potential value was a mere sideshow to their real concern, which was the fate of their friends and elders, Sal and Joe.

"Why does there always have to be something?" she asked her husband. "Can't we ever just have a normal life?"

Doug didn't answer right away. He didn't have an answer. This summer was to have been the start of a normal life for them both.

"I don't get it either," he finally said.

Then he squeezed her hand and led her away from the rock toward an outstretch of beach that had been exposed by the minus tide of the day. For the next hour, they walked quietly; stopping to study the occasional tidepool before walking on towards the next freshly exposed treasure.

They found an old rope that was still in good condition. It looked like something used to tie up ships or barges and had a large loop in each end as well as a couple of iron hooks, one of which was attached to a two-foot section of iron chain.

"I can use this for sure," Doug said, as he helped Mara drag it along the beach.

The rope was heavy, obviously washed in by the tide, and too nice to leave unclaimed. When they got back to the SUV, they hoisted it into the back section, trying to shake as much sand out of it as they could, before calling Thor to them.

They watched as Thor situated himself on top of the coiled treasure, and then climbed back into the vehicle for the short drive home.

"Derrk says that the fishing season went really well and he'll have the final numbers to me next week," Doug said, breaking the solitude. "If the numbers come in as good as I think they're going to, maybe we should take a trip over to Juneau just to get some hours onto the Cessna."

"I wonder if Joe would want to go with us?" Mara asked.

"We'll make sure that he does," Doug told her. "Della should be able to help with Beachmoppers while we're gone, and I'll put Dennis in charge."

"That's a good idea," she said. "I need to get out of here for a while."

"Me, too," Doug said, squeezing her hand again. "Trouble is, it'll all be waiting for us when we get back—but the break might do us both some good, and maybe it'll help Joe out some, too."

Chapter Thirty-Four
Juneau

The Cessna flew like a dream. Even Joe Michael had to admit that, despite knowing that Doug had just passed his flight exam and had precious little experience with piloting a plane in the steep mountains, unstable weather, and windswept currents that made flying in Alaska especially challenging.

Unknown to Joe, Mara had completed a flight course and also passed the exam, so it was hard for her to contain her smile when she mentioned that fact halfway over the Gastineau channel as they approached Juneau's Hoonah airport.

When she finally turned around, Joe Michael was staring blankly out the window.

"You heard me, didn't you, Joe?" she asked him.

"Huh?" he answered.

"I was telling you that I took the flight course and passed the exam along with Doug."

"Oh," Joe answered.

Mara turned around. She watched as Doug lowered the Cessna carefully downward and silently practiced the sequences in her head as he went through the steps for a careful landing.

"I think we should sleep at home tonight and get up early to hit Costco and do our other shopping," Doug said. "That okay with you, Joe? You can open up yours and Sal's place or just bunk at our place."

"Okay," Joe answered.

They had no sooner climbed into the cab at the airport, when Joe wanted to stop at a nearby convenience store. While they waited, Doug and Mara decided that they should start leaving one of their vehicles at the airport now that they had a plane and would be flying back and forth.

Joe seemed as uninterested in that information as he had in the rest, so they drove straight home, stopping only to pick up some burgers on the way.

"I'll be fine in my own place," Joe said as they walked the boardwalk to their cabins.

"Well, if you're sure, Joe," Mara said.

"Goodnight," Joe answered before opening the door to his cabin after fumbling for the key in his pocket.

Mara saw the tip of the feather lift out of Joe's pocket for an instant, and she saw him touch it gently before pushing it back inside.

"Do you need any blankets? I know that Sal packed up just about everything . . ."

"Goodnight, kids," Joe answered, before walking into his cabin and closing the door behind him.

When Doug knocked on Joe's door the next morning, it took several minutes for the old man to answer. When the door finally opened, he could see that Joe was not only rumpled and tired looking, but that there was the unmistakable odor of alcohol on his breath.

"You go on ahead," Joe said. "I'm not feeling that well."

"Maybe some breakfast would . . ." Doug began, but before he could finish, the door clicked closed, leaving him to stand drop-jawed at this sudden change in the old man's behavior.

The scenario played out in much the same way over the next two days. Even Mara could not get the old man to leave his cabin.

By the fourth day, both Doug and Mara had grown so concerned that they feared that they would have to do something radical to get Joe Michael moving again. Was he even eating? Neither of them had ever seen him act this way.

They were sitting on the deck looking over the harbor when they heard someone walk through the house. It was Joe Michael, looking like his normal self—clean shaven, dressed neatly, and shuffling along in his usual manner. In his hand he held his phone.

"Got a cup of coffee, Mara?" he said softly, as if there were nothing at all unusual going on.

Mara got up and made coffee for the three of them, brought out some cinnamon rolls to snack on and sat down without saying anything.

"She really laid into me," Joe said.

"What do you mean, Joe?" Doug asked.

"Sal. She laid into me a good one. Said she was comin' back and that I darned well better not be doin' what she thought I was doin' or there'd be hell to pay."

Chapter Thirty-Five
Sal Returns

It was as if Sal's trip and Joe's additional trip to Rhinebeck had never happened, the way the two of them jumped right back into the life that had always been their norm.

The flight back from Juneau had been as smooth as the flight there, and this time Joe even pretended to be impressed with Doug's flying skills and Mara's diligence in coaching him.

Sal was waiting when they got back, and by the looks of things, completely her old self.

"What the hang, Donald, Darrell, Denton—"

"It's Dennis, Mrs. Michael," the exasperated summer worker said more patiently than most would have. "Perhaps Mr. and Mrs. Williams can explain everything about the bowl to you."

"Yeah, perhaps!" Sal sniffed before stomping off while muttering something under her breath about the colossal waste of time they were all spending on a worthless piece of pottery that even the dog wasn't impressed with."

Still, despite her misgivings about the situation with the bowl, the fact that there was solid evidence that it was a priceless artifact did not escape her attention.

"So, Darrell—"

"It's Dennis, Mrs. Michael."

"Whatever," Sal dismissed him. "You say that you've got the true blue goods on this bowl so as ya kin prove it's ours?"

"I do, Mrs. Michael," Dennis answered.

He began explaining the entire sequence of events leading up to the discovery that the bowl was valuable, including the photos, glazing, offer of his father to handle the case without charge, and the letter from the Director of Museum Affairs in Honsu, Japan.

"And, if that is not enough to convince you, then I think you should see this."

Dennis took Sal into the back room where he kept all the files and photos of the tsumani debris. He pulled up a chair to make her as comfortable as possible, and then proceeded to insert a flash drive into his computer, turning it towards Sal and adjusting the screen so she could see it.

Minutes later, the replay of the breaking news bulletin by Elzianne LaMonte played across the screen.

"I don't need to see any more," Sal said in her perfect Sylvia LaMonte speech pattern, then she abruptly got up and left the room, leaving Dennis Connor to wonder what had just happened.

Mara was the first person to see her leave.

"Sal, you look upset."

Sal brushed past her and began arranging things on the tables inside Beachmoppers.

"Sal, what's wrong?"

Sylvia LaMonte stepped back, squared her shoulders, brushed a wisp of gray hair back from her face, and began walking towards the door. Then, just as abruptly, she turned and walked back to Mara.

"I thought I could bury the past," she began. "Then, when I went back to Rhinebeck, it was all still there."

She went on to explain her meeting with Monsignor St. Jean, his death, the box with his belongings, the key, the safety deposit box with the envelopes, and her surprising—even to herself—rejection of Joe Michael.

"The first time, it was just me being scared to face him; scared to let him know who I really was, and scared just because I felt scared," she said.

"Is that why Joe was so upset?" Mara asked.

"Well, it was a good enough reason if you ask me," Sylvia answered, "But I talked to him and we spent some time together—some quality time like we haven't done in a long while."

Sylvia paused and smiled at the recollection before continuing.

"The second time, though, was a total collision of circumstances. When I think of how my poor husband must have suffered after having shared such closeness with me, and how hard it must have been for him to be rejected so publicly, well, words can't even express . . ."

"He didn't talk about it to us," Mara said gently. "And then there was the episode in your cabin back in Juneau."

Sylvia took her by the hand and walked her over to the waiting area of the now closed Beachmoppers showroom. There she sat on one sofa, facing her friend on the other.

Slowly, she retold the story of missing the deer, landing in the ditch, thinking all was fine, and truly not remembering her recent past when her husband arrived for dinner.

"I didn't piece it together for weeks," she said. "Not until people started telling me bits and pieces of what happened. Later, I went in for a CT scan and they found a small clot pushing on my brain. I guess it happened during the accident. I spent another week in the hospital while they treated me with blood thinners. I'm still taking them now, matter of fact."

"Wow!" Mara said softly.

"Then, after a week or so, my memory came back just as fast as it had left. That's when I called Joe. I was shocked to hear him like he was—speech slurred, despondent—not my husband at all."

"We were worried, too," Mara said.

"I've never known Joe to drink," Sylvia said. "I mean, we'll have a beer or a cocktail out socially once in a while, but never any serious drinking. To hear him that impaired was shocking. That's when I knew I had to snap him out of it."

Mara laughed limply. "I heard about the phone call."

"He gets despondent sometimes," Sylvia said. "The war, the fire, Stu. Sometimes it all gets him down, but never have I known him to drink himself silly like he did during those few days."

Mara squeezed Sylvia LaMonte's hand.

"It's been hard on us all," she said. "It's like all our lives have been turned around with learning who you really are. Don't get me wrong, I'm so glad that we know the truth, but the adjustment has been hard—maybe because of all that's gone on before, you know. Maybe that's why Joe left instead of . . . "

Sylvia LaMonte stood up, leaving Mara sitting on the sofa.

"I know, dear. I know. Now, if you'll excuse me, I've got to find my Joe and maybe take a walk, or go to bed early, or do something that feels even remotely normal for just this short moment before I have to think about all this again."

"Goodnight, Sylvia," Mara said.

"Goodnight, dear."

Chapter Thirty-Six
Time Now

S al found Joe in the yard where the landing craft was unloading. He had already summoned Mara and Doug as well as all available support staff.

"Be sure to hang a closed sign on Beachmoppers," he told Dennis, the last person left to notify. "And if you'd be good enough to pick up my niece, Della on your way down here, I'd be grateful."

Once they arrived, Mara and Doug took charge so that Joe could rest, directing the crew on where to stack the loads of debris they had brought in.

"It's pretty chop chop out there already," the captain of Beachmoppers said. "I was relieved I was able to get the landing craft in like I did, but the load is relatively light and this craft's as good as they come, so here we are."

The debris was the usual assortment of floats and broken furniture—nothing of real value as it now stood, but they had found an artist who was creating an entire line of saleable items by reconstructing the furniture fragments into useable art pieces and donating a percentage of the profits to disaster relief efforts in Japan.

"Why don't you two just let us handle the rest of the unloading?" Doug asked the elderly couple.

Joe Michael didn't resist. His face sagged in a way that added about ten years to his appearance, and the twinkle in his eye was gone. Mara watched Sal stare at her husband as he walked around the yard. For a moment, she caught Sylvia LaMonte's eye in a moment of knowing concern of their shared love for the old man. She started to move toward him, but stopped as Sal gently placed her hand into his and led him toward their truck.

"We'll be fine, Joe," Doug said.

Joe Michael climbed into his dualie and waited while his wife climbed into the other side. Then he drove off—slowly, purposefully, and without looking back.

Later that afternoon, Doug and Mara saw the dualie parked outside the elderly couple's house. They didn't stop in as usual and neither did Sal or Joe come to the window as they usually did to see who was there.

Inside, Joe Michael napped in his recliner as Sylvia LaMonte stared at the manila envelope she had left tucked into a corner of the bookcase across the room since first discovering it in safety deposit box 7 at Rhinebeck State Bank.

After a while, she got up and brought it to the table. Perhaps it was time to face the inevitable task of opening it and really examining the yellowed papers it held.

She peeled back the flap and started to remove them, then abruptly got up and began pouring a cup of tea from the water that simmered on the woodstove.

She stopped to pull a comforter over her sleeping husband, making sure that his feet were tucked in tightly, and smiled as Joe moaned a soft thank you. Then she walked to the window letting herself become overly engrossed in watching a ship sail by.

The sun was sliding toward the horizon when she sat back down at the table and pulled several pieces of paper out of the envelope and spread them across the table.

She got up and made herself another cup of tea, tucked the blanket more tightly around Joe's shoulders, then sat back down. Among the papers, in a small, tattered envelope, yellowed with age, was a letter. Handwritten, the cursive script that was almost lyrical in its presentation caught her eye. She picked it up and began to read.

Chapter Thirty-Seven
The Letter

Dear Fr. St. Jean,

For eighteen years I have cared for the gardens of this parish and many of those adjoining estates, all the while carrying the burden of being forced to conceal what no man should have to hide.

Although I might well have chosen to unburden myself in your confessional, knowing as I do that you are bound by the laws of God and the Church to retain my strictest confidence, I chose instead to try to right the wrong I have done in the best way that I know how.

I do so with the greatest confidence that you will allow this letter to find the persons who it can most help piece together and repair the damage my act of concealment has wrought on their lives.

It is to you, a man of integrity and a man whom I trust, that I leave this letter, knowing that somehow, and perhaps long after I am gone, you will find a way.

You will now know, as I have recently learned, that I have terminal cancer and will likely be gone before Christmas. It is thus my dying wish that you be the first to know the truth and the last to set it free.

Elzianne Jeanette LaMonte is my daughter borne of a lifelong and passionate affair with her mother, Melinda LaMonte, wife of Johnson LaMonte.

So that all should know, both Mellie and I went to Johnson LaMonte when she first learned she was carrying my child. They should also know that in keeping with his wishes and in order to ensure the best possible future for our child, we ceded to Johnson LaMonte's insistence that the world should never know that the child was not his own.

In return, my darling Mellie and I physically parted ways as she acceded to Johnson LaMonte's other condition that they remain married, as to not do so would have jeopardized his standing as a leader within both the Rhinebeck community and the very tightly knit parish of St. Aloysius. It was the beginning of the end of my life that we did so, even though she incurred my undying gratitude when she saw to it that over the years I was able to watch our daughter grow up.

Johnson died without revealing the truth to Elzianne. To ensure that the truth would never be disclosed, he left a stipulation in his will that if it ever were revealed, or if any evidence of a resumption of a relationship between Melinda and me should occur, the substantial inheritance left to both Melinda and Elzianne would be cut off.

To accomplish this, he engaged the trust of his best friend, Jameson Kindle, to whom he entrusted official oversight of his estate—a fact that Melinda LaMonte found increasingly repugnant as the years went on.

Despite the risk, Melinda and I managed to meet secretly a few more times. It was during one of those times that she revealed her intention to find a way to punish Jameson Kindle for his willingness to try to control both her wealth and her happiness.

When I spoke to her for the last time before she died, she told me that in an effort to protect our daughter, Elzianne, she had initiated a series of events that would tarnish the legacy of Jameson Kindle and his heirs in such a way that her financial assets and those of our daughter, Elzianne, would forever remain secure.

Later, when Melinda and Johnson's eldest daughter, Sylvia, married Jameson's eldest son, Bert Kindle, Melinda stepped up her efforts to destroy Jameson Kindle by tarnishing the good name of his firstborn son, even despite the fact that he was now married to her eldest daughter, Sylvia.

Jameson Kindle died soon thereafter, but not before he began to suspect the plot that had been unleashed against his son, Bert, and warned him accordingly.

When Sylvia LaMonte Kindle began to suspect that her mother was sabotaging her husband, Melinda denied it, while secretly increasing her attack on Bert Kindle. When Sylvia confronted her mother once more about her suspicions, Melinda tightened her hold on the family fortune by implicating Sylvia in what we know were trumped-up attempts to discredit Bert, and equally trumped-up allegations that Sylvia was somehow responsible for her husband's untimely death.

It was at that time that Bert and Sylvia fled Rhineback and began a new life in Alaska, where they lived until Bert Kindle died, and after which I lost track of her whereabouts.

A few years later, Melinda learned that she, too, was dying. She summoned me to her bedside for what I thought would be our last passionate goodbye. Instead, she told me that our daughter would carry on her mission to discredit Bert Kindle's name after she was gone.

Although she then swore for the last time that she loved me, when I objected to her plan for Elzianne, she went on to say that our daughter had always been told that Johnson LaMonte was her father, and would never learn the truth about me from her, thus dashing any hopes that our daughter would know my love for her.

And in her chilling last words to me, Melinda told me that she had already warned Elzianne that there was a man who had been trying to extort money from her by claiming to be her father, and that that if that person ever came forward, she should pursue legal action against him.

It is with a heavy heart that I now go to my own grave knowing that my daughter will never know the love that her mother and I shared, and through which she was conceived, while also knowing that the woman I loved betrayed me, just as she did her own husband, in the end.

I only ask God's forgiveness for my sins and pray that somehow after I am gone the truth can somehow be told.

Most sincerely,
Henry Wilson Patterson

Chapter Thirty-Eight
In Face of Reality

S ylvia (Sal) LaMonte Kindle Michael was asleep sitting bolt upright in her chair when Joe Michael found her in front of the window around 3 a.m. For a moment he feared she was dead. Never had he seen her this way.

Carefully, he gathered the pages of the letter from the floor and set them on the table before leading his still sleepy wife to their bed. When she had rolled over into peaceful slumber, he returned to the place by the window and read the letter.

How had Sal carried this burden for so long? He knew that she had been married to Bert Kindle and he knew that the marriage had been a happy one. He also knew that Bert had died unexpectedly and that Sal had taken to living near the sea—moving from seaport to seaport—until meeting and marrying him in what she told him had been years since Bert's death.

The whole thing about Rhineback, the LaMontes, her mother, and Elzianne were new information. As far as he knew, much of what had just been revealed in this letter would have come as a surprise even to her.

As far as Elzianne, Sal had once mentioned that she had a sister, who she had lost track of over the years—something she had also told him was A-okay with her as the two of them had never been close. But the fact that she had carried the knowledge that her own mother was trying to sabotage her life must have been almost more than she could bear. And now to learn that Elzianne, her lifelong nemesis, was only her half sister, well . . .

How selfish he had been to assume that his life's burdens outweighed hers. No wonder she had been acting strangely as of late. How unforgiveable that he had fled Rhinebeck assuming that she had rejected him and had not searched for the truth about his wife.

Unable to sleep and consumed with shame, he wandered about the house, as if in doing so some answer to all of this would present itself. Perhaps all this was only a dream. When he tripped on the stoop between the living room and the new addition that led to the kitchen, he knew it wasn't.

The first hint of the sun's arrival appeared as a thin yellow line along the horizon when he finally decided to make himself some coffee. He watched a ship sail by, then another, before getting up to pour himself another cup of the comforting brew.

Sal's footsteps in the other room told him she was up, so he poured a cup for her, too.

"I read it," he said gently when she appeared.

"It's good that you did," she answered. "I really don't think I can face this alone any longer."

Chapter Thirty-Nine
The Check

Sylvia had told her husband about safety deposit box 7 after her first trip to Rhinebeck, and about how the contents had come into her possession. Joe hadn't asked about them since. If they had stayed hidden away forever, he might not have cared, but here they were, splayed out in front of him, along with all they represented.

He picked up an uncashed cashier's check. It was dated more than forty years ago and it was signed by Jameson Kindle, identified therein as executor of the estate of Johnson LaMonte—Sylvia's father. The amount was staggering, especially for its day. It was made out to Reverend Father St. Jean on behalf of St. Aloysius Parish for one million dollars. When he turned it over, he saw that it had been endorsed to Sylvia LaMonte.

Joe handed it to his wife.

Sylvia was aghast. What favor had Jameson wanted from Monsignor St. Jean? Had he tried to buy his silence over something that might have been said in the confessional by Johnson LaMonte, or perhaps even by her mother, Melinda LaMonte?

Sylvia knew her friend well enough to surmise that he would never have broken his vows as a priest to reveal anything he had heard in the confessional. J.T. had always, since their childhood, been both a humble and an honorable person.

The evidence within her hands seemed compelling. Had Monsignor St. Jean never cashed the check so as not to expose the attempted bribe and place himself or the parish in jeopardy? Further, he had signed it over to her. Had he done that so that should it ever be discovered, it could never fall into the hands of Elzianne, Dorland, or anyone else, and would go directly to her, thus providing her with at least a share of her parents' wealth?

Why hadn't he just destroyed it? Wouldn't that have been the easiest thing to do? Instead he had secured it in his safety deposit box for all these years. Had he tried to find her? No one else had succeeded in doing so after Bert died, so it came as no surprise that he, too, would not have found her—that is, if he had been looking.

Of this she knew she could be sure, J.T. would never harm her or be a party to anyone who would seek to harm her. How hard it must have been for him to carry this burden for his entire life, to risk his own career, his life's vocation, to hold onto these things for a lifetime.

Their affection for each other had been real, their friendship deep, starting from when they first met on the playground in second grade, and ending only with his death. It had transcended time, and their life choices. It had been above all else, pure. Free from pretense, devoid of pretext, greater than worldly needs.

He was in heaven; of this she was sure. No amount of manipulation, no level of conniving by her family, and no faltering in faith and commitment had kept him from his path.

She had been fortunate to know him—to have earned his friendship and his loyalty. She would protect him and his good name in return, no matter what came of the contents of the envelope laid out before her.

Chapter Forty
Another Letter

The letter addressed to Doug and Mara Williams from Dorland Kindle was point blank. An investigation was being launched into the death of Bert Kindle and the distribution of all assets that were in his possession at the time of his death were being scrutinized to ensure that they had fallen into the hands of their rightful owners.

Pursuant to this end, be advised that no further activity should be undertaken using either the F/V Driftfeather or the F/V Storm Roamer.

~Dorland P. Kindle, Attorney at Law
Kindle, Kindle, Chase, Swanson, and Fitzlander, LLC

"Ignore it!" Dennis Connor Sr. barked into the phone after receiving a fax of the document at his Boston office. "It's nothing but intimidation."

"But can he freeze the use of the seiners?" Doug asked, as he huddled around the phone with Mara, Sal, and Joe.

"Just carry on with your business," Dennis Sr. answered, deflecting the original question. "I'll be firing off a strongly worded note to Dorland Kindle today."

~ ~ ~

"We were approached by a private vessel yesterday at which time they handed me some kind of document stating that I must cease further operation of both seiners," Derrk Stanley told Doug during a satellite call from somewhere in the Gulf of Alaska.

"It's nothing like you're thinking—is that all they said?" Doug answered.

"That's all," Derrk replied. "Look, Doug, I've known you a good long time and long enough to be sure that you'd never intentionally get yourself tied up in anything even remotely suspect. Still, this is over the top and nothing I've ever come across in all my years on the seas before. If there's something going on—if you're in some kind of trouble, or something—well, I just can't let myself get caught up in it, you know."

"What're you saying, Derrk?"

"I'm bringing the seiners and the fish in until you get this straightened out, Doug. That's all I'm saying."

Derrk paused for a long silence before speaking again.

"Look, we've got our quota for the year already, so the rest is gravy anyway, man. Just call me after you straighten it out, okay?"

"Sure. Do what you have to do, Derrk. I appreciate you getting the boats back in and finishing up with the catch you have on board."

"We should be coming in sometime tomorrow," Derrk answered. "Into Juneau, I mean. We'll offload there and I'll tie the seiners up in their usual places."

"Okay, Derrk. I'll get your pay out to you and the crew as soon as we tally things up." "As much as I appreciate that," Derrk said, "If you need the money to . . ."

"I don't need the money, Derrk," Doug shot back, fighting to keep any tension from showing in his voice. "You and the crew will be paid on time."

"Thanks, friend," Derrk said before ending the call.

"Son of a . . ." Doug said out load, shoving his boot hard into a piece of rotted log that marked one of the parking places near Beachmoppers.

The force of his kick sent pieces of wet, splintered wood flying in all directions, leaving a pile of debris in a five-foot radius around the log. He found a rake and cleaned it up, forcing himself to nod and smile at a passing tourist, before raking the splinters into the woods.

He'd be talking to Dennis Connor Sr. first thing tomorrow. But right now it was 3 p.m. Alaska Time, which meant that Connor's law offices would be closed.

The seiners would be fine in Juneau. He had been thinking of pulling maintenance on them anyway.

Dennis Connor Sr. had told him not to worry. He would try not to, but what the heck. Did he really need this right here and right now?

Chapter Forty-One
Had Enough

Sal found Mara sitting in the dark lobby of Beachmoppers.

"It'll be dark during the day soon enough, Jane," she barked.

Mara turned slowly, her face drawn; her shoulders slumped.

"They're trying to take the seiners."

"Who's 'they,'" Sal bellowed.

"Elzianne LaMonte and Dorland Kindle," Mara answered. "I know you know about this."

"Ain't no one takin' nuthin'," Sal said. "Now buck up, Jane, and let's get this shop opened up."

Mara grabbed the arm of the sofa and stood up, tears streaming down her face. "I can't take any more . . ."

"Buck up, Jane," Sal repeated. "No one likes a sniveler."

"Stop it!" Mara screamed. "Stop it! Stop it! Stop it!"

"Get a grip, Jane," Sal shot back.

"Did you hear me? I said stop it!" Mara repeated, her tears now flowing so hard that her body was wracked with sobs.

Sal stepped back and said nothing. She had never seen Mara this way. She began uncovering tables in the gift shop, trying to think, while Mara sobbed uncontrollably.

"Forget about this. Forget about these stupid tables, and this stupid junk, and all the stupid tourists," Mara sobbed.

"Now jest a danged minute here, Jane," Sal said.

"Did you not hear me?" Mara said, grabbing a cloth from Sal's hands and throwing it in a heap onto the sofa. "I asked you to stop it."

Before Sal could say anything, Mara continued.

"Stop it! Stop all of it! Stop acting like you don't care about any of this, stop patronizing me, and most of all, stop the charade. Stop the charade and lose the Sal character while you're at it."

"I don't like seeing you this upset," Sylvia LaMonte replied, forgoing her persona as Sal.

"Really?" Mara screamed. "Really!"

Sylvia LaMonte stepped back.

"You don't like seeing me this upset? You don't like driving your loving husband Joe around the bend with trying to figure out who you are? You don't like seeing my hardworking husband lose his livelihood? Is that what you don't like, Sal—Sylvia—or whoever you are at any given moment?"

"I'm not sure I deserve this, Mara."

"And I'm not sure I deserve this either, Sylvia. Nor does Doug, or Joe, or anyone else you've been lying to all this time."

"Is that what you think? That I lied to each of you?" Sylvia said softly.

"What else do you call it?" Mara shot back. "Of course you lied. Your whole life's been a lie from what I've seen."

Sylvia clutched one of the table covers to her breast, her face drawn, pale, and coldly real.

"That's enough, Mara," Joe Michael said from the doorway.

Mara sat down. In all the time she had known Joe Michael, he had never spoken to her this way.

Joe Michael walked over to his wife and gently helped her to a chair, while Mara looked for a tissue with which to dry her eyes and blow her nose.

For several minutes, no one spoke. Then Joe said, "We're going to New York—all of us."

"What's going on?" Doug Williams said as he walked into the room.

Chapter Forty-Two
Shopping

Mara sat back as the plane lifted off. Taking a commercial flight to Anchorage had been a snap decision she had made after calming down, getting a good night's sleep, and agreeing with Doug that they should all think this through and be ready for the trip to New York.

Even Joe had agreed in the end.

"You've got the clothes we bought when you first came back," she had heard Sylvia tell him, then adding, "and we can pick up some more when we get there."

"I'll shop for Doug up in Anchorage," Mara had said, and so off she had gone.

Sarah had agreed to drive down from Palmer to meet her. Having worked for several years for a major fashion house in New York, she would know exactly what to pick out for her best friend to take on the trip.

Meanwhile, as the plane lifted above the clouds, Mara reflected on her outburst of yesterday. She had been uncharacteristically hard on Sal and uncharacteristically open about her feelings. Strangely, though, she felt little regret.

She had always tried to be a team player—to be the facilitator and to go with the flow. She had occasionally shown a feisty side, but the events of the past few years after her husband Brad's death had made her more introverted.

Even knowing that she had Doug's love forever hadn't seemed to be enough to bring her out of her shell. She had believed him when he told her that leaving her was the worst decision of his life, and she believed him now when he said he would never leave her again, but she had long ago learned that terms like "never" and "always" were sometimes relative to circumstances that no one could foresee, and so though she loved her husband with all her heart, she kept a small part of it hidden securely away from everyone just to protect it from being forever and irrevocably crushed.

She was sure that Doug sensed this, just as she knew that it made him try harder to please her, but he had told her on more than one occasion that he understood and would spend the rest of his life regaining her trust.

Even her friends had let her down, though she had long ago chosen to forgive them. They had been the best they could be under each and every circumstance, and she knew full well that she, too, had sometimes let others down, so she had chosen to move on from holding any grudges.

Her dog, Thor, was her truest friend and confidante. He had been with her since she had first arrived in Alaska and their bond was tight and true. Even Doug, who was Thor's original owner, had mentioned how close Thor was to her, but hadn't it been Thor who had led him to Mara in the first place—on that stop in Wrangell, when she had first come up on the ferry? It was she who had insisted that Thor go with them to New York, no matter how inconvenient tending to him there would be. He was her dog and where she went, Thor went, and that was that. And so she ordered him a beautiful silk-covered collar from a place in New Jersey as well as a collapsible canvas crate in which he would be secure both during travel and while in hotel rooms. Then she got his paperwork in order, his immunizations up to snuff, and all this she had accomplished before stepping on the plane to Anchorage this morning.

Chapter Forty-Three
Anchorage

For that one sunny day in Anchorage, Mara and Sarah shopped with the laughter and abandon that had been their norm in college.

Mara tried on every possible combination of clothes in their effort to find the perfect look for her trip to New York and finally settled on a handful of outfits that were versatile enough to mix and match at will. Their biggest dilemma became shoes. She hadn't worn anything but sensible shoes for years and totally resisted moving back into the discomfort of city shoes. She finally found some, though, and had to admit that they looked really good and weren't really all that hard to walk in.

Sarah made her stop at the make-up counter, too. Although Mara had a natural beauty, Sarah convinced her that she would seem out of place in the sophisticated world of New York if she were to dress too plainly. They also stopped at a high-end hair salon and were lucky, as they were able to get in with one of the top stylists, who had just had several cancellations due to an accident causing an unexpected closure of the highway north of town.

The cut was flattering, leaving her hair between chin and shoulder length, and using a clever set of angles that made it look flattering whether she wore it straight or in its natural curly state.

After stopping for lunch at a quaint little bistro by the Inlet, they made their way back through the shops at the Captain Cook Hotel, and then down 4th and 5th Avenues, stopping at the 5th Avenue Mall and then crossing over to Nordstrom's.

Mara picked out several pair of pants for Doug, as well as an array of dress shirts. He had a couple of nice sport coats that suited him well already.

They stopped on the children's floor to pick up some new things for B.D., too.

"Anna's babysitting him today," Sarah said. "He's almost too big for her to pick up, but she does a pretty good job of keeping tabs on him."

Mara smiled at the mental image that flashed of young Anna corralling the rambunctious B.D.

"Couldn't you just come up for tonight?" Sarah implored. "Ellie's ready to pop. Her due date is next week. And Ben is waiting on her hand and foot. You'd smile if you could see how happy they are together."

"They both deserve it—to be so happy," Mara said. "After all they've been through."

"Everyone misses you and Doug, Mara," Sarah said. "We all love you both so much."

"I know," Mara answered, a wistful glaze coming across her face. "I know, but right now I have to take care of my own life—and Doug's, and Sal's . . . and, of course, Joe's. They need me now, but tell everyone we'll see them all soon."

"I understand, Mara," Sarah told her. "I guess I'd better head back to the Valley."

"And I've got a plane to catch," Mara answered.

Mara took a shuttle to the airport. There was no sense in making Sarah fight all the Anchorage traffic and it would help her get on the highway before rush hour stole an entire extra hour out of her day.

"I'll call soon," Mara called as her friend drove off, "Promise."

Chapter Forty-Four
Kismet

T he day in Anchorage had worked its magic and given Mara a chance to step outside of the furor that had once again enveloped her life. Why was there always something—and not insignificant somethings either? Was this perpetuation of chaos and unrest her new normal? Should she be afraid to ever relax and feel happy again for fear that some new crisis would emerge?

Ever since receiving the feather on the ferry a few years ago—well, even before that, really—starting with Brad's disappearance in the plane crash, her life had been one series of unexpected dramas after another. No, she couldn't blame the feather. This had all started before the feather. And she couldn't blame Alaska, or the people there, who were now her life. What, then, could she blame? Destiny? Karma? Both?

She watched the shoreline as the plane began its descent into Hoonah. Thank God she had everyone here to lean on. What if she had been forced to go through all of this alone? It was true that some of her stress was because of events surrounding her new friends and loved ones, yet she had learned early on that her own life was already entwined with theirs. Coincidence? In retrospect, probably not. Just the fact that Brad had talked of Alaska so often now seemed like kismet that had brought her to where she was today.

As the plane approached the runway, she thought she could see Joe's dualie on the road leading to the airport, and was that Doug's truck right behind him? It sure looked like it. If kismet had brought her to Alaska and if kismet had brought her the love of people like Joe, Sal, and Doug, then she trusted that this same kismet would continue to protect her and those she loved, no matter what circumstances life might toss her way.

When she stepped off the plane, there they all were at the window of the terminal, Joe, Doug, Sal, and Thor. When she walked through the single door inside, they hurried to embrace her and help her with all the bags she had brought back from Anchorage.

She had instantly noticed that Sal was there—kind of a surprise after the harsh way Mara had chastised her.

"Sal," she began, looking apologetically into her friend's eyes.

"Are ya gonna worry about somethin' ya spewed from yer heart or are ya gonna just accept yerself and accept the love we all got fer ya and that nothin' ya can do will ever drive away?" Sal whispered into her ear.

Doug took the shopping bags from her arms as the two women shared a warm embrace.

"How about some lunch?" he said.

"That sounds like a pretty good idea to me, too," Joe added.

Chapter Forty-Five
Airborne

When the four of them left for the Lower 48, even Doug had to admit that it was an ambitious undertaking to fly nearly three thousand miles to New York, especially for a novice pilot such as he. But Mara could fly, too, and would serve as a backup navigator. Joe was coming along, and he had plenty of flight experience, and so they had taken on the task, studying charts and maps for the month before leaving, equipping the plane with every possible navigation device and plenty of emergency supplies.

They had shipped a lot of their supplies ahead of them to a friend of Sarah's, who would store everything until they arrived. The biggest concern, actually, had been the wisdom of taking Thor, but Thor was as much a part of them as anyone, and so he came along.

If New Yorkers didn't like Thor, that was just going to have to be their problem as individuals. His travel crate would fit in the back of any rental vehicle they would choose, and Mara had bought a cooling pad for the crate to help offset the high temperatures there. She had also obtained a health certificate and some added immunizations for the trip—for things like parvo virus, kennel cough, and other contagious dog diseases, and of course, his travel certificate for Canada.

And so, on a drizzly day in late August, Dennis Connor drove them to the airport and handed the luggage from Doug's pickup over to him so he could load the plane, finishing with lifting Thor's crate inside, where Doug strapped it to specialized hooks that he had installed in the floor of the tail section.

After Thor had been lifted and secured inside his crate, Doug helped Joe and then Sal into the plane, making sure that they were comfortable and secure. Then he and Mara did one last walk-around before climbing in themselves.

They had already decided to spend the first night in Ketchikan, which meant that when they had barely gotten going, it was time to stop again. It was a special stop just for Sal. She had some business regarding the deed to Beachmoppers that she wanted to finalize there. While she and Joe were gone, Doug and Mara walked Thor, gave him food and water, and then walked around town, stopping for a sandwich along the way.

The ferry was in port, a sight that sent a mixture of chills and trepidation up Mara's spine as she remembered the nearly one year that she had fled from port to port on the ferry system.

"Seems like a lot has gone by since then," Doug mentioned, as if reading her thoughts.

Mara smiled a half smile as Doug squeezed her hand. After they had finished eating, they untied Thor from a post outside the restaurant and continued on their way.

By late afternoon, they had met up with Sal and Joe again. They found a motel room that would accept dogs and checked into their respective rooms before walking to a nearby restaurant for dinner. Once again, Doug tied Thor up outside, only this time the restaurant manager told him that he would have to take Thor around back because one of the tourists had complained about the restaurant allowing a dog by the outdoor eating area.

"I'll just take him back to our room," Doug said. "He's gonna have to get used to the crate life anyway."

When Doug returned about twenty minutes later, their order was just arriving. The food was good and well worth the wait. The thing with Thor—well, they were on the road, so they had better learn to adjust.

They lingered over another glass of wine and then dessert before returning to their rooms. Doug and Mara found Thor sound asleep inside his crate, but he woke up readily when they walked in, so they took him for a stroll along the waterfront, enjoying the brightness of the moon against the water.

"Once this is over, I think life is going to be just fine," Doug told Mara. "We've been through worse than this. Pretty soon we'll be taking walks like this every day. You'll see. I've just got a feeling about it."

Mara didn't answer as she leaned into her husband and walked along, while Thor circled around them and then ran ahead before coming back and circling again.

After a hearty meal the next morning, they were in the air and on their way to Prince Rupert.

Chapter Forty-Six

Prince Rupert

It wasn't often that the regulation stop at Canadian customs was tedious, but for reasons everyone privately hoped was not a portent of things to come on this trip, the officials on duty decided to empty the entire plane.

"Typical," Joe Michael sputtered as he walked with Sal and Mara to an indoor waiting area that would keep them out of the heavy rain.

"Really?" Mara asked.

"If they can mess with Alaskans, then that's what they love ta do," Sal spewed. "Danged righteous, bureaucratic, tight as—"

"I guess they're just doing their job," Mara said, in a weak attempt to dispel any friction between Joe, Sal, and the customs official, who was leading them toward the customs building.

Once inside, they provided their passports as well as the required documentation for the plane. Although everything involving Thor's paperwork was in order, they still brought him out of the plane, with one agent snarling something about wolf-hybrids.

"I think our documentation will show that we are certified to own and transport—" Mara said, but the official just kept walking as if he didn't hear her. "But, sir—"

"Ma'am, consider yourself fortunate that we aren't going to find a reason to seize the animal right now," he sternly interrupted her.

"Thank, you, sir," Mara replied, biting her tongue to keep from telling the official that if he made one false move towards her dog that he'd be dealing with her as well.

"It's not the first time they've acted like jerks to Alaskan pilots or tried to throw their weight around with the passengers," Joe said quietly when Mara entered the building. "In all my years of flying, my one dream was to never have to fly through Canada again."

"Well, I know a lot of Canadians that are very nice, although I know what you mean about how some of them treat Americans."

She paused as her mind drifted back to the service station whose staff had refused to serve her in the Yukon several years ago during her move to Alaska. If it hadn't been for Doug's intervention, she might have had to stay hungry till the next stop some hundred miles down the road.

"I guess they've had reason to be thorough," Mara said in the way of trying to dispel any tension. "You know how all the fringe people seem to come here and all."

The three nodded in silent agreement. It was true that every adventure seeker, every person on the run, every near-broke runaway seemed to find his or her way up to Alaska for some reason.

"Might as well take it in stride," Sal said, adjusting the fit of her shirt.

If they were lucky, no one would find the pistol she had tucked down into her cleavage. If they weren't—well, no sense borrowing trouble.

"Your plane's just about ready for you to reboard," the customs official said, looking up from his intense focus on his computer as Sal turned to face him after tugging on her blouse to make sure that the gun didn't show.

Fortunately for her and her travel companions, she had not triggered anyone into making a decision to strip-search a nearly eighty-year-old woman, because if they had tried, well that would be a story unto itself.

When the three travelers reached the Cessna, Doug was just lifting the last of their luggage into the plane.

"We'll talk about it later," he said, before anyone could say anything.

"You're cleared for takeoff," the customs official told him, "or there's a motel down the road about a half mile if you feel like staying over. As long as the plane stays here and we keep the keys, there'll be no added delays in the morning."

"Thank you," Doug replied, "But we'd just as soon get moving on."

Even though the stop had set them back four hours and he was exhausted from re-loading the plane for the second time that day, there was no way Doug was going to stay in Prince Rupert.

For the next hour, sensing his frustration, no one said anything. Mara stared out the window, Sal read, and Joe Michael simply sat there, finally reaching into his pocket and feeling the feather resting there before picking up the newspaper that Sal had left in the seat pocket the other day. As the plane lifted off, leaving Prince Rupert behind, he proceeded to read yesterday's news.

Chapter Forty-Seven
Destination: New York

Six days later, with the rest of the journey remaining uneventful, they landed at a private airport that advertised it was open to the public. It was small, rural, and only a few miles from Rhinebeck.

Doug had arranged to have a rental car waiting for them and they had already made reservations at the motel where Joe had stayed on his earlier trip.

The plan was for Sal and Joe to mingle with some of Sal's old friends around Rhinebeck under the guise of being there for a vacation. As Sylvia mentioned to the church secretary at lunch a few days later, "While I'm here trying to honor my good friend, Monsignor St. Jean, I want to retrace the steps of my youth before it's too late for me to travel anymore, but first we must get things rolling with his memorial."

The truth was, that even though this was a fact-finding mission under the guise of a vacation, it did not take away from the fact that Sylvia LaMonte Kindle Michael had every intention of following through with a fitting memorial to Monsignor St. Jean. After all, he had been the loyal spiritual advisor to everyone in the parish for his entire adult life, and he had also proven to be her true and loyal friend. The least she could do would be to see that he was honored in return, and in a way befitting the sacrifices he had made to remain in Rhinebeck—sacrifices not obvious on casual observation, but that those such as one who had been raised there could understand so well.

Although Joe had agreed to attend several social functions with his wife, he was also determined to help Doug in any way he could, so he rented another car for his wife and gave her the keys before preparing to take off with Doug to the New York's capitol city of Albany, about an hour away.

"We should be able to research just about everything we need to in the way of licenses, death certificates, wills, and just about any kind of public record we can find on the LaMonte and Kindle families," he told Joe. "I've done plenty of that kind of research—you know, deep research on titles, laws, and the like for the fishermen's lobby."

"Should be interesting," Joe replied, reaching into his pocket to feel the security of the feather. "I just hope we don't learn about more than we can handle."

"Well, first, let's just see what we can dig up."

Doug wanted to say more, to get Joe thinking along more positive lines, but the events of the last few years had taught him to dismiss nothing. Nothing was impossible. Nothing would come as a shock, no matter how surprising it might first appear. And so, too, nothing would deter them from their mission to exonerate Sylvia LaMonte, and free her from the lifetime of repression her mother and sister had inflicted on her tender spirit.

And Mara needed to know some peace. They all did. No, he would not be deterred from digging up anything and everything he could in clearing up this latest assault on their well-being. He owed it to his wife and to himself. He owed it to Joe and Sal, and most of all, he owed it to all the people that Elzianne LaMonte had tread upon in this life.

"We can drive back here every night, or we can just find a room in Albany and let Sal and Mara do their own thing," Doug mentioned to everyone over dinner that evening.

By the time dessert had been served, they had all agreed that Sylvia would remain around Rhinebeck, Doug and Joe would do research in Albany, while Mara would go to New York City, where she would stay at Sarah's friend's apartment and do some investigating of both the New York Cultural Museum, and a certain Elzianne Jeanette LaMonte. Fortunately, Sarah's friend would be gone on assignment to Europe for Mara's entire visit, leaving her free to come and go as she pleased from the upscale loft in the TriBeca section of the city.

Thor would stay at the motel with Sal. He was safe there and everyone else felt better knowing that he and Sal would take care of each other while they were out doing their thing.

Chapter Forty-Eight
New York, New York

New York City was the polar opposite of Hoonah, Juneau, and even Bellingham, but Mara quickly learned to find her way around the well-run city.

She spent the first couple of days getting acclimated—stopping for a bagel and espresso each morning, reading the many newspapers that were available on virtually every corner, and otherwise allowing herself to sink into the culture of the area.

She called Sarah several times, and for about half a day, the two thought that Sarah might be able to join her in the city, but B.D. suddenly came down with a fever, and so Sarah needed to stay in Palmer to take care of her son.

Doug called every evening so the two could stay up on what each of them was doing, and even Sal called once and reminded her to avoid making eye contact with New Yorkers even though it was such a natural part of Alaska living.

"Jest don't do it, Jane," Sal barked. "If there's anything that'll tag ya as a danged touri, it'd be that."

On a sunny Wednesday morning two days later, Mara went to the New York Cultural Museum, paid the $27 admission fee, and signed the guest book as *Mara Benson Williams, Juneau, Alaska* (including listing her email and phone for notification about future promotions), a notation that did not go unnoticed by the museum attendant, who was a tall, thin, well-dressed woman with a nametag that read *Julia Bruce.*

"I nearly visited Hoonah this past year," she said in a soft, well-modulated voice.

"I'm sorry that you missed the opportunity," Mara answered.

Suddenly, Julia Bruce became all business.

"May I direct you to a specific area of the museum?" she inquired.

"I'd like to visit as much as I'm able to today," Mara answered. "Do I begin here?"

Julia Bruce personally accompanied Mara to the elevator, suggesting that she begin on the third floor.

"Being that you are visiting from Alaska, you may find this exhibit quite interesting," she said. "Once you are finished there, we have an unusual collection of rare porcelains from around the world, including a rare Edo Period Japanese porcelain that I believe was found somewhere near where you live."

Julia Bruce pulled a small piece of paper from her pocket and studied it.

"Yes, it was found in Hoonah, Alaska—near Juneau," she said stiffly.

Mara fought to maintain her composure, brushing her hands down her calf-length white trumpet skirt as if to straighten any wrinkles, before adjusting the matching peplum jacket.

"Why, thank you, Ms. Bruce. That does sound interesting," she said, forcing a smile.

"Please let me know if I can be of further assistance," Julia Bruce replied.

For both women, the encounter had been surprisingly stressful, although neither could be sure just why. It was with a great sense of relief that Mara watched the elevator door close, and with a subsequent sense of trepidation, watched it open again on the third floor.

She silently thanked Julia Bruce for having given her the heads-up about the display, for there, in every direction she looked, were artistically arranged pieces of what looked like the very tsunami debris that Sal and her company had been collecting all summer.

She looked around to see if anyone was looking, even scanning the ceiling for cameras that she felt certain were there, before discreetly taking several photos of the exhibit with her smartphone. Almost immediately, she emailed them to Doug—just in case anyone decided to confiscate her phone or something.

Feeling jittery as she did took her back to her days on the run from the South American drug cartels, so she didn't linger, taking a stairway down to the next floor, glancing back over her shoulder several times as she hurried along.

She walked slowly through the area, before suddenly locking her gaze onto a solitary exhibit within a circular glass cage, before which stood an armed guard.

"My, but how lovely," she whispered to the guard, who showed no sign of emotion and instead stepped backward slightly to allow her to view the contents of the glass case.

There, inside the tubular floor to ceiling enclosure, stood a tall pedestal that held one single object. It was Thor's water bowl.

"All of this for one bowl?" she said, trying to engage the guard, but he stepped back into position again, not responding, and not allowing his gaze to meet her own.

"May I?" she asked, taking her smartphone from her purse.

"Of course, ma'am," the guard replied.

And so she took pictures of the bowl from several angles, including one that captured the unique dip in the glaze that assured her that the bowl was Thor's water bowl. Then she emailed the photos to Doug and to the Dennis Connors—both junior and senior—went down to the lobby on the elevator, bade her goodbye to Ms. Bruce, and hurried back to the apartment still trembling inside at what she had just seen.

Chapter Forty-Nine
Collaboration—of Sorts

When her cell phone rang the next morning, Mara wasn't sure whether or not to answer. The caller ID said *private caller* and she had long ago learned to be cautious about opening herself up to those she didn't recognize.

"Hello," she said, silencing the ringtone of Hawaiian music that was meant to keep her in a positive state of mind.

"Is this Ms. Williams?" a woman's voice said.

"This is Mara Williams," she answered.

"Pardon me for disturbing you, Ms. Williams, but this is Julia Bruce from the New York Cultural Museum. You know—from yesterday?"

"Yes, Julia. Did I forget something?" Mara said, before taking a deep breath and hoping against hope that this call was not about the photos she had taken inside the museum while there.

There was a long pause before Julia Bruce spoke again.

"I know that you do not know me and—I hope I am not intruding by suggesting . . ."

As Julia Bruce paused, Mara could hear a deep sigh.

"Would it be an imposition if I asked you to meet me for lunch this afternoon, or as soon as it is convenient?" Julia Bruce said after regaining her composure.

This time it was Mara who hesitated.

"I know this seems unorthodox and forward," Julia Bruce continued, "but I have some information that I would like—that it is imperative that I share with you. Information that will be of interest to you and your friends who operate Beachmoppers in Hoonah."

"But how . . ." Mara gasped.

"I'll explain at lunch," Julia Bruce replied. "Can we meet at two at Chez Maison de Soleil? It's about thirty minutes from you, but the food is worth the long drive. And don't worry about a cab, I'll send a driver to pick you up from a location of your choosing."

"A driver won't be necessary, although I do appreciate the consideration," Mara answered. "I'll see you there at two."

"Yes, two," Julia said before hanging up.

~ ~ ~

Chez Mais, as the locals called it, was indeed one of the finest restaurants Mara had ever visited. Thankfully she had followed Sarah's advice and dressed in a conservatively upscale urban manner.

"Hello, and thank you for coming," Julia Bruce said as she stood and shook Mara's hand.

"It looks like the pleasure will be all mine," Mara answered coyly. "At least I hope this is mostly social."

"I'm sorry to say that as much as I would like to get to know you better, my reason for asking you here was to somehow present to you some information that I feel you should have."

Mara was worried enough to order both a glass of wine and a small salad instead of one of the grand entrees she had wanted to try.

"Well, then I guess I'm all ears," Mara answered. "Please begin, Ms. Bruce."

"For more years than I can recall, I served in the position of first assistant and executive secretary to a woman named Elzianne LaMonte," Julia Bruce began. "But when I was made to realize by her own actions that she had been taking unfair advantage of me for all those years, I left her employ and took the job as museum attendant."

At the mention of the name, Elzianne LaMonte, Mara was fully tuned in to Julia Bruce and whatever she had to say.

"Do you know her?" Julia asked.

Mara nodded. "Slightly. Please go on."

"At the time that I left the employ of Ms. LaMonte, she was preparing for a lengthy stay in Hoonah, Alaska, for the purpose of scouting for and buying tsunami debris from the earthquake in Japan. That's how I discovered Beachmoppers. Do you remember taking a call about a large party wanting to visit? About six months ago? You emailed me your contact info then."

Mara nodded again, as if to indicate that she remembered, but the truth was that she fielded several calls a day about summer reservations and apparently there had been nothing about this one that had made it stand out in her mind.

"Because my only daughter had been planning her wedding for close to two years, and because Ms. LaMonte chose to callously disregard the importance of yet another major event in my life, I decided I had had enough of her selfish and self-centered ways and decided to leave," Julia Bruce continued.

"First I made all of the travel arrangements that were necessary and then I left her employ and went on a two-week vacation to Hawaii. I had no sooner returned and taken this new position when the tsunami debris began coming in.

"At first it seemed essentially uninteresting from an artistic viewpoint, but then when she brought in the Edo period porcelain, I became very intrigued, especially when someone from the expedition—someone who had been there the day the bowl was, shall we say, 'found', and a former coworker—took me aside and said that Ms. LaMonte had stolen the bowl from the yard in front of Beachmoppers."

Mara could feel the blood draining from her face. She glanced quizzically at Julia Bruce, then downward. Picking up her fork, she pushed her salad around on her plate, took a sip of Malbec, and looked squarely at the stranger who had just presented her with the gift of the truth.

"Am I to understand that you have definite knowledge that the dish was stolen?" she asked.

Julia Bruce opened her purse and removed a small card upon which she proceeded to write the name and phone number of the person who had witnessed the theft.

"My friend, Claire, will help you. We have already discussed it," Julia said. "But please, I want to caution you to be careful. Elzianne LaMonte is a shrewd and ruthless person. Claire has come forward at great risk to herself. Please do all you can to protect her."

"And yourself?" Mara asked. "Why are you doing this, and most importantly, will you be safe?"

"There is little else that Elzianne LaMonte can do to hurt me," Julia replied. "I have less than three months to live according to my doctors, who tell me that the cancer was so advanced by the time I sought treatment that there is little they can do."

Mara reached across the table to lay her hand on top of Julia Bruce's. The woman looked healthy as best as she could tell, but still, she had no reason to doubt what she was being told.

"It's brain cancer," Julia said, sensing Mara's skepticism. "They say I'll be pretty much normal until the tumor begins to invade key areas. I know that right now I look normal, and although I am beginning to have symptoms, it would serve no real purpose to burden you with those right now. Please trust me. This is something I had to do to try to stop Elzianne from hurting anyone else. You seem like a nice person. Please treat this as a gift to me—the gift of allowing me to right one wrong before I die."

With that, Julia Bruce rose from the table, steadied herself for a moment, gathered her things and walked away.

"The check has been taken care of," the server told Mara a few minutes later. "Please enjoy your day."

Chapter Fifty
Seeking Serenity

S tunned by what she had heard from Julia Bruce, Mara wandered the
streets around Chez Maison de Soleil for the rest of the afternoon, stopping in the many shops and boutiques along the way to try to—as she told
Doug on the phone—equalize.

She had already left a message for Julia's friend, Claire, and left her the
number for Dennis Connor Sr. as well as mentioning her desire that Claire
contact him with her information ASAP. She had since received a text from
Dennis Connor Sr. saying that he had been contacted by Claire and had
taken a deposition from her.

Doug had told her that he would be talking with Dennis Connor Jr. about
correlating his own photographic evidence with his father and Dennis, Jr. had
returned a text saying that his father had also taken a deposition from him
regarding what he had witnessed while working at Beachmoppers.

The rest could wait for now, and so she wandered and shopped, even taking
a walk along the Hudson River. How strange to see a river confined within
the cement walls of skyscrapers, overrun by bridges, its banks lined with miles
of barges and freight docks.

She had seen rivers this way much of her life, but after having lived in
Alaska and having seen them in their natural state, the sight left her shaking
her head at the way the earth had been violated. She had never considered
herself an environmentalist per se, and it could be argued that progress and
development had benefitted her as much as it had the rest of mankind, but
she still loved to see the wild rivers—essentially untouched by man in any
kind of permanent way, and so the walk did little to soothe her psyche.

She got back to the TriBeca loft around six, having picked up takeout on the way there. She ate out on the balcony, watching the hustle and bustle of the traffic move by on the street below. It created a monotonous din against the emerging coolness of evening. She tightened the sweater she had thrown over her shoulders and when that wasn't enough to ward off the evening chill, she stuck her arms into the sleeves and buttoned it up.

Strange to feel so cold here when she was from Alaska, but the humid air, mixed with the smells of the city and her own fatigue had lessened her tolerance for discomfort. When a chain of police cars and rescue vehicles roared by, piercing the dusk with their shrill and distressing squeals, she went back inside, pulled the curtains, and made herself a cup of hot tea.

Doug wasn't picking up his phone, so she texted him a message that she was going to go to bed early and would talk to him in the morning.

After tossing fitfully for close to an hour, she got up and wandered around. There was a guitar on a stand in a corner. Why should it hurt anything to pick it up? She strummed a few cords, tuned it, and began playing in the classical style that she favored. Playing guitar had always relaxed her. Before long she felt drowsy enough to try to sleep again. This time, with the song *Lullaby* playing in her head, she closed her eyes, not opening them again until the hubbub of morning's traffic woke her once again.

Chapter Fifty-One
Albany

Joe Michael found doing research in Albany almost as tedious as he did being within the confines of a big city. Even Juneau, as active as it could be with its influx of cruise ships and tourists in summer, and legislators meeting at the capitol in winter, did not feel this oppressive—or this old.

It wasn't that the city lacked appeal. It had a rustic quality despite its size, but buildings taller than four to five stories blocked the sky and the sun. A person couldn't even watch the weather come in, and the scurry for cover he saw among the people when rain began to fall amused him. What made them so afraid of a little rain?

The city was neat and tidy, with a colorful and obviously historic past. The two rivers that intersected there provided a soothing backdrop for the lush greenery, too, but the housing, although neat and charming, was far too dense for the tastes of a man who had spent the majority of his life in the Alaska wilderness, and the houses lacked the individuality of Alaska homes, leaving an impression of sterility of spirit.

The people he met there were friendly enough, although much less willing to engage with strangers than would ever be the case in Alaska. No, Joe Michael was an Alaskan and for that he was grateful. If nothing else, being here in Albany, and around Rhinebeck and other eastern cities had given him a deeper appreciation of just who Sylvia LaMonte was as a person, and of what influences had formed her character.

He had married Sal Kindle, but he had been forced to see the woman he loved as more than the crusty persona he had always taken at face value upon discovering that her real name was Sylvia LaMonte. Although the knowledge had left him uneasy, and somehow wondering if the two of them could really continue in the way they had thus far, he had pledged his love to her and she to him.

The person she was inside was the person he loved, no matter which way she chose to present herself outwardly. This much he had learned, and so he would stay in Albany with Doug to research her past and to clear her good name. He would visit Rhinebeck whenever his wife felt the need, and he would cherish the fact that even though he was well into his 70s, life still held surprise and adventure for an old man, who had been born as an Alaska Native and who had been fortunate enough to have lived close to the earth for most of his long and interesting life.

"Could use a cup of coffee," he told Doug.

"Me, too," Doug answered. "And maybe a bite to eat."

Chapter Fifty-Two
Turbid Turbidity

During his research at the library, Doug had discovered all the evidence he needed to help bring forth the truth about the Kindle and LaMonte families, including proof that Melinda LaMonte had changed her will just three months before her death—a time during which, according to Sal, her mother had suffered a stroke that had affected her ability to speak, and had left in question her ability to understand the spoken or written word. Prior to that, Sylvia and Elzianne had been slated to share their mother's estate equally, but as it turned out, the new will had left the majority of the fortune to Elzianne.

According to an affidavit provided to Melinda LaMonte's attorneys by Elzianne just four months before her mother's death, a private investigator hired by Elzianne LaMonte had submitted a statement alleging that Sylvia had revealed the truth about Melinda's relationship with Henry Wilson Patterson to her and Bert's attorney after her husband, Bert Kindle, had revealed it to her.

The divulging of this information had violated the stipulations set forth in Johnson LaMonte's will, and thus had put both Melinda and Elzianne at risk of losing their inheritance.

This had been discovered when a series of letters written between Jameson and Bert Kindle had been intercepted by Driscoll Kindle, who was at that time in the process of assuming control of the estate from the terminally ill Jameson. Those letters, which included Jameson Kindle's sentiment that by putting this all in writing, there could never be any confusion about his intent after his death, had been included in the report on file from the private investigator.

Apparently Jameson Kindle had revealed the truth to his son, Bert, in a fit of conscience—a surprising shift for a man whose own head had so been turned by the charming Melinda that he had been blind to her attempts to implicate the son he was now confessing to.

In the correspondence with his son, Jameson had made it clear that he had already turned over the management of the secret and the estate to Driscoll due to his pledge to monitor Johnson LeMonte's estate.

"Loyalty to a friend is priceless," he had said, "and a man cannot claim friendship to one to whom he cannot be loyal. I must warn you though, that Driscoll will aggressively pursue Johnson LaMonte's instructions."

Jameson had further advised Bert that he and Sylvia would be wise to retain the secret of Elzianne's parentage, pointing out that Sylvia's inheritance had been generous and unexpected, and to reveal the truth would be to risk the furor of Elzianne LaMonte, who was as devious, desperate, and conniving as her mother.

"Be assured," Jameson had written, "that Elzianne LaMonte will stoop to any low to protect her interests. You have little to lose by remaining quiet, but Melinda and Elzianne have everything to lose if the truth about Elzianne gets out."

Although the revelation had ultimately gone no further than Sylvia and Bert Kindle, the fact that it had the potential to be revealed had frightened Melinda and Elzianne, who stood to be discredited as legitimate heirs if the truth should become known.

With Melinda being on her deathbed and now at risk of losing everything she had spent her life fighting for, her lawyers had drawn up a new will to protect both Melinda and her love child. That will had been registered thirty days before the death of Melinda LaMonte. Jameson Kindle had died shortly thereafter, never having been told by Driscoll that Melinda had learned of his betrayal.

Doug had also uncovered proof that during this time Sylvia LaMonte and her husband, Bert Kindle, had been out at sea and that even after learning of the change in the will, had taken no steps to challenge it.

Coincidentally, both Bert Kindle and Melinda LaMonte died soon thereafter, leaving Elzianne an heiress and Sylvia a grief-stricken widow, who had shown no inclination to engage with her sister or to challenge the new will, even though records would show that her inheritance had been a fourth of what Elzianne had received.

Even now, Doug scratched his head as he tried to remember how it had all come together, and how he had been left with the shocking realization that all of the hostility and suspicion about the Kindle family and about Sylvia LaMonte had been nothing more than a smokescreen generated by Melinda LaMonte to cover up the truth about Henry Wilson Patterson, and to protect her own interests.

In the end, Melinda LaMonte had been backed into a corner from which only a devious and conniving plot of desperation could help her retain her husband's wealth for both herself and for her illegitimate daughter.

Presumably, because of his love for Melinda, Henry Patterson had never questioned the facts that Melinda presented to him, and had remained silent as she requested out of loyalty to her. He had, via his silence, allowed Johnson LaMonte to claim the child that he knew was his own, knowing that this would protect Johnson LaMonte's status as a conservative leader in the tight-knit community of Rhinebeck, where although such things happened, they were never openly discussed. It could also be presumed that the fact that his daughter would now enjoy a life of privilege served as an additional incentive.

In the end, Henry Patterson, like Melinda's daughters, had come to realize that he had been nothing more than a pawn in her grand scheme to retain her position as the rightful heir to Johnson LaMonte's assets, but the knowledge did little to dampen his love for the mother of his only child. His confession, left in the hands of Father St. Jean, had been his only revelation of the truth and the only unburdening of his soul.

Doug's discovery of all this had been mind-boggling enough, which made it all the more unbelievable when he found a certified copy of adoption papers, which showed that a woman named Sylvia Kindle had given up a daughter to a couple from Boston thirty-eight years ago—a time frame which coincided with the time that Melinda LaMonte and her daughter Elzianne had ramped up their assault on Sylvia and during which time Sylvia's husband, Bert Kindle, had died.

Doug could barely absorb this. Besides learning of the turbid past of the LaMonte family and those close to them, another previously unknown fact about Sylvia LaMonte had now emerged. Who could then blame her for having assumed a new identity, yet, what else was out there left to be discovered about Joe Michael's wife?

"You look like you've seen a ghost," Joe Michael said.

Doug backed out of the screen that showed the adoption papers, but not before emailing a copy to his phone. Joe could not know about this right now. Maybe there was a mistake. Why couldn't he think?

"I'm just tired, Joe," he lied. "My head is splitting. Let's stop for today and go find something to distract us—maybe a movie or a couple of drinks or something."

"I could use a day away from all this," Joe answered.

"You drive, okay?" Doug said, surprising the old man.

"Yeah. Sure. No problem," Joe answered.

Chapter Fifty-Three
Jane

Doug had already called Mara and asked if she wanted to come back to Rhinebeck for the weekend as he and Joe had decided they needed a break from all the research. When he called Sal to tell her to expect Mara about midday, Sal told him about the busy weekend she had planned. The committee that had formed to erect a memorial to Monsignor St. Jean was holding a fundraiser on Saturday evening that would feature an auction as well as local entertainment.

"We're all coming in Friday afternoon," Joe said when he talked to his wife a while later. "I guess we're available to help with the fundraiser if you need us." Indeed she did need them, if for nothing more than to have some familiar faces around. Sal's stay in Rhinebeck so far had been pleasant, but she felt alone and off her turf, and she missed her husband as well as the young couple that she and Joe called "the kids."

By Friday evening, everyone had gotten together at the restaurant across the street from the motel and had filled each other in on what they had learned. Since everything was now in the hands of Dennis Connor Sr., now was a good time to sit back and wait. Helping Sal with the benefit for Monsignor St. Jean would be a nice diversion. So would some quality time between Sal and Joe, as well as Doug and Mara.

That night, Doug looked at Mara as she slept. He had told her everything except for what he had learned about Sylvia LaMonte having given birth to a child thirty-eight years ago. He wasn't sure why he chose not to tell her that. Right now, there were a lot of things he wasn't sure of.

He had decided not to tell Joe either. He needed some time to think this through—to think of any and all ramifications. Besides, was it really any of his business if Sal had given birth thirty-eight years ago? It looked like it had been right about that time when she lost Bert and her mother. Maybe she had been overwhelmed, thinking she had no money. It could have been a lot of reasons. At least she had realized her limitations and given the child up for adoption.

He could ask her about it, but was it his place to do so? If she had wanted him to know, she would have told him. And Joe—maybe Joe already knew. Who was he to try to determine what information was private between a husband and a wife?

It wasn't until later, when he was scrolling through the files he had sent to his phone from Albany, that he scrolled past the adoption papers again. He went to the lobby while Mara slept and hooked his phone up to the computer there, downloading and enlarging the file. He then printed it on the printer provided by the hotel and began to study the document.

The child had been a female, born in May and given the name, Jane, with the last name left blank. The mother was listed as Sylvia Anne LaMonte and the father as Bert Kindle (deceased). There was a notation that the child should not be told of the adoption and that Sylvia's name would not be revealed to the birth parents or to the child. In a special notation, Sylvia LaMonte did request information about the adoptive parents and retained the option to contact them at a later date if she so chose. Otherwise, the adoption would be a private matter with her identity sealed for a time frame of thirty-five years.

On closer scrutiny, Doug saw that a new birth certificate was attached to the original one that had the identifying information for the birth parents hidden. The print was so small, that he couldn't make it out, so he found a copy machine in the lobby and blew up the print so he could read.

A Boston couple with the same name as his wife's parents had adopted the child. How odd. Benson wasn't that unusual a name and when he googled the names of the adoptive parents, he found four others by the same name in New England alone. The child's birthplace had been Bellingham, Washington, which came as no real surprise since Sylvia and Bert had been working in the Gulf of Alaska and other parts of the Pacific Northwest. But then he saw the one entry that made him gasp. The child's birthday was the same as Mara's!

This could not possibly be true—or could it? Hadn't it been odd that Sal had popped into Mara's life when she needed her the most? Hadn't she always affectionately referred to Mara as "Jane"? Could Sylvia LaMonte be his wife's birth mother? In all he and Mara had been through, in all the strange things that had faced, never, ever would he have imagined this scenario.

He tucked the papers inside the breast pocket of his jacket and zipped it shut. Then he tiptoed into his and Mara's room taking Thor out of his crate as quietly as he could.

"Where you been, Doug?" Mara said sleepily.

"Just downstairs for a beer," he answered. "Thor wants out. I'm going to take him for a walk and be back in about a half hour."

"Okay. Be careful. Turn your phone on," Mara said, rolling over. "Turn mine on, too, before you leave, okay? Just in case . . ."

Doug did as his wife asked and walked with Thor to the door.

"See you in a bit."

Chapter Fifty-Four
Saturday

M orning came too soon for a guy who had spent the past few weeks traveling and had been awake most of the last two nights.

Doug Williams had skillfully avoided the routine questioning of his wife, who wondered if anything was wrong and just why he hadn't been able to sleep last night.

By 9 a.m. he and Joe had helped the church custodians set up tables and chairs in the church hall, rope off a section for the auction, and prepare two tables near the entry where tickets would be sold and flyers for the event handed out.

Sylvia LaMonte had been smart in suggesting that visitors be provided with both printed invitations and donation envelopes for the event, as well as with a separate flyer that gave the highlights of Monsignor St. Jean's years at St. Aloysius.

As he watched Sal and Mara work to set up the entry tables, Doug couldn't help but make new comparisons between the two women. If there was any physical resemblance, he couldn't see it. Sylvia LaMonte was a full head shorter than Mara and lacked her lithe gracefulness.

Maybe there had been some mistake and Sal had given birth to another daughter with the same name as Mara's parents, who had been born on the same day as his wife. Could the use of the name Jane, which had first appeared on the original birth certificate, also be mere coincidence?

As the two women worked silently side by side, he couldn't help but notice that there was something different in how they interacted. He had first seen it when Mara had snapped at Sal back at Beachmopper's one afternoon after Sal's identity as Sylvia LaMonte had been revealed.

Since then, things had been congenial enough, but still there was a reserve between them that hadn't been there before. Perhaps it was an issue of trust—a suspicion about a woman who had claimed to be someone totally different in name, actions, and demeanor from everything she had seemed to be.

Whatever the case, there seemed to be a cooling of the lighthearted banter that usually marked conversations between the two, but no cooling of their affection for each other. Both had made that abundantly clear.

As he continued to work around the church hall, he watched the two women work side by side, wondering how long it would be before they would work things out. He didn't have to wait long.

Two of Rhinebeck's finest socialites were standing outside the restroom door, where he was working when he overheard them making snide inferences about Sal. Suddenly Mara walked past them into the restroom, apparently also overhearing some of their conversation—at least, she scowled and hesitated slightly before continuing inside.

Before he could even process it all, Mara came back out and calmly stopped to chat with the two women as if they were long-lost friends.

"Sylvia LaMonte is a doer, isn't she?" he heard Mara say. "For someone of her caliber to return to this place that has done so much to detract from the happiness of her life—she truly has pulled off a remarkable feat in organizing this fundraiser for the parish priest who served this community under the same oppressive elitism that Ms. LaMonte was raised in. Wouldn't you agree?"

Mara paused, smiled, and made direct eye contact with both women, who looked at each other in obvious discomfort at the inferences.

Then, not missing a beat, Mara said, "Sunday New York Times social page—well, so many times that I can't recall all of them. You did follow her story, didn't you?"

Casting knowing looks between themselves, the two women didn't respond. "I thought so," Mara said, before walking away.

"Why are you so red in the face, Jane?" Sal said, out of earshot of the others once Mara returned to their table.

"Nothing, Sal. How about if we put the brochures here and set up a collection box for donations for those who prefer to make a contribution that way?"

Sylvia LaMonte let the matter drop. Her eighty-some years on earth had taught her that sometimes it was best to just leave well enough alone.

Maybe later she'd talk to Doug about the distance and the coolness she had been noticing. She'd think about it some more.

Chapter Fifty-Five
Sunday Brunch

Doug tossed and turned most of Saturday night, finally falling into a deep sleep around four. Mara woke him at nine so he could shower and get ready to meet Joe and Sal in Rhinebeck for brunch. If anyone noticed, no one mentioned the deep circles that had formed under his eyes, or the sallow color of fatigue that his skin had taken on.

Sal and Joe had just been to mass at St. Aloysius when they met at a small, popular breakfast spot near the church.

"I don't know what you said to those two old crones who would trip on their own broomsticks if they ever had a kind word to say," Sylvia whispered to Mara as they were seated, "but they both came up to me this morning and invited me to lunch before I leave town, and said that they personally wanted to thank me for my generosity and leadership in spearheading the memorial drive for Monsignor St. Jean."

Mara glanced at Doug, patted Sal on the hand, and simply smiled.

"I'm really thinking pancakes," she said.

"Pancakes for starters," Joe laughed.

Doug was the only one who didn't order a full country breakfast, opting instead for black coffee, toast, and oatmeal.

Mara glanced at him more than once. Something was wrong. What could it possibly be? She knew better than to press him too hard. He would tell her when he was ready; otherwise, if she pushed him too hard, he would just clam up all the more.

Doug barely touched his oatmeal, and finally, after about fifteen minutes got up, excused himself, and said he had forgotten to walk Thor before coming to the restaurant, and would be right back.

When he returned about thirty minutes later, Joe was getting ready to pay the bill, and Mara had gone up to purchase some pastries for later. He told himself that now was just as good as later.

"Sal, I wonder if you'd mind going for a walk with Thor and me? There's something I want to talk to you about."

"Sure," Sylvia LaMonte answered.

"I'll see if Joe will take Mara back to the motel for now and I'll be right back," he said.

Joe would have no part of leaving the two of them possibly stranded in Rhinebeck. With their motel a good ten miles away, he told Doug that he wanted to show Mara some of the things he had discovered about Rhinebeck.

"And I've been looking for a minute to talk to Mara alone for quite some time," he added. "About the feather, you know, if the opportunity comes up."

"Sure, Joe. Perfect," Doug replied.

While Doug and Sal stayed behind, Joe proceeded to escort Mara out of the restaurant. He was straightforward with his message, pulling the feather from his pocket and placing it into her open hand, before gently closing her fingers around it.

"I understand now," he said, "Why the feather came back to me."

Mara nodded.

"I'm not saying I understand everything, or that there won't be any surprises ahead for me, although at my age, you'd think I'd seen just about everything by now," he chuckled.

Mara opened her hand and stared at the feather that had been a part of her life since before she had even set foot on Alaska soil.

"It's like we can never be free—really free," she told Joe Michael.

"But you're wrong, Mara," Joe answered. "The feather is just a symbol of your own inner strength, like it somehow makes you feel you are protected, when all the while you are becoming stronger and more able to protect yourself."

"Is that how you see it?" she asked the old man, who had looked after her ever since her own father died.

"It's the way I've always seen it," Joe said. "Even when I didn't know what I was seeing."

Mara laughed a hollow laugh.

"Now, what kind of sense does that make?" she said, squeezing his arm.

"Just as much sense as life itself," Joe answered. "Now you keep this feather. You're young, with your life still meant to be long, while I'm old and realizing that I grow closer to my end time on this earth every day."

Mara tensed. "Is something wrong? Are you sick?"

"No, Mara," Joe Michael said. "Nothing like that. I'm just old, that's all. And none of us is meant to live forever, not me, not you—no one. It's just that I'm farther along in the process than you are, that's all I'm saying. Just farther down the trail."

"Before, when you gave me the feather, things happened to me," Mara said, treading cautiously into areas she wasn't sure she really wanted to visit.

"Yes," Joe nodded.

"Do you think—are you saying—or feeling, like something is going to happen to me, that for some reason I'm going to need the feather?" Mara asked.

"No. Don't get paranoid," Joe said.

"But—"

"Look, Mara, it's just time, that's all. Sure, stuff's going to happen to you, you wouldn't be living a normal life if it didn't, but I'm not sensing anything or feeling some vibe if that's what you mean, unless loving you like a daughter is causing my sensors to go askew. Come to think of it, after all we've been through, it's a wonder that either of us can claim anything normal about our senses, you know."

Suddenly Mara hugged the old man. She wrapped her arms around him and hugged him with everything she had. Slowly, he lifted his arms and hugged her, too.

"I'll be here for you as long as I walk this earth," he told her, "but one day when you least expect it, I'll be called home to be with the Lord and when that day comes, I want to die knowing that you have a piece of me with you here on earth—to take care of you, like I promised your father I would do. You keep this feather safe. Now c'mon, I want to show you those violet houses that Sal showed me."

Chapter Fifty-Six
Blast at the Past

Sylvia LaMonte watched as Doug Williams took the maitre'd aside and pointed to a secluded booth near a large bay window in the corner of the restaurant. When he returned, he leaned over and took her coat from the place she had laid it on the seat.

"I know I mentioned going for a walk, Sal," he said, "but if you don't mind, could we move to the booth in the corner? We can talk there, over coffee."

"Sure, Doug," Sal answered in a manner that was unusually docile for the old woman.

She followed as he worked his way between the tables to the booth. There he waited to seat her, gave them a moment to order coffee, and began.

"I don't know how to bring this up. I don't even know if it's my place or my business to bring this up," he began.

Doug paused to wipe his brow. Why did it feel so hot in here?

"What's troubling you, Doug?" Sylvia LaMonte asked him. "I could see that you weren't yourself during brunch. Is everything okay between you and Mara?"

"Yes. Everything's fine. Look—Sal—Sylvia—"

Doug stopped to sip his coffee. Why was this so hard? Suddenly he unzipped his breast pocket, removed a fold of papers from it, and handed them to Sal.

She said nothing as she read, sifting slowly through them without even the hint of expression on her face. Doug sipped his coffee and signaled for the server to bring more.

Finally, after studying the papers for what seemed like a full fifteen minutes, Sylvia LaMonte spoke.

"It's true, Doug."

He couldn't believe his ears. After thirty-eight years of carrying this secret around and at least the last five in the company of her own natural daughter, Sylvia LaMonte sat there with all the aplomb of a national-level stateswoman.

Doug was lost for words. How unbelievable was this life going to get? How many more surprises did it have in store for him and Mara? He wanted to get up and walk out, but somehow managed to stay.

"Sal," he said. "You mean to tell me you're just going to sit there and tell me it's true—like this bombshell that's been dropped on me is just a pebble in the big blue sea of your life?"

"I've known for a while, Doug," she said.

Doug stood and paced around the area near their table.

"Is everything alright, sir?" the server asked.

"Yes. Fine. Check, please," Doug told him.

"I'll meet you outside," he told Sylvia.

For once the old woman said nothing. She sat and watched Doug as he made his way to the cash register, not waiting for the server to bring the bill. Then she gathered up her coat, purse, and the umbrella she had brought because of the threat of rain, folded the papers Doug had presented her with into a neat bundle, and made her way outside.

Together, they walked silently along the river, while Thor bounded ahead off-leash.

Despite angry looks from a couple of passers-by, he didn't call the dog back to him. Thor knew how to behave and would stay away from people. Just for show, though, Doug let Thor's folded leash dangle from one hand.

"I figured it was only a matter of time," Sylvia LaMonte said, "before this would all come out."

"I don't get you, Sal," Doug said, stopping suddenly to face her. "You could have just lived out your life with no one the wiser, but for some reason, for some reason that I just cannot fathom right now, you decided to come into the life of a young woman—a woman that you abandoned at birth, and who has suffered so many losses over the course of her life—and complicate it all the more."

Sylvia LaMonte stared at the ground. It was obvious that Doug's anger was affecting her, and why shouldn't it? Everything he was saying was true.

"I can't deny any of it," she began.

"Deny what?" Doug interrupted her. "Deny that Mara is your daughter? Deny that you've known it for years and never tried to let her know? Deny that you could have left her alone to protect her instead of coming into her life like some kind of ghost from the past?"

Shoulders squared, jaws clenched, and feet planted firmly on the ground, Doug again faced Sylvia LaMonte—standing only inches away. Without the false bravado of her Sal persona, the old woman looked small and frail.

"And what about Joe? Is he in on this, too?"

"No!" Sylvia said with a sob. "He doesn't know. No one knows but you."

Doug walked ahead, called Thor to his side, and snapped the leash onto the dog's collar before turning back.

"I don't think I can talk to you anymore right now," he told her.

When he looked up, Joe and Mara were driving slowly in their direction.

"Get in the car before it rains," he said, his voice softening only slightly. "I'll catch up with everyone later."

"But what should I tell them about you and Thor?"

"Tell them whatever you want to," Doug said. "You'll think of something. You're good at lying."

Chapter Fifty-Seven
Last Piece of the Puzzle?

One of the custodians from St. Aloysius saw Doug and Thor walking alongside the road and offered them a ride. Even though he said he was only going three miles, Doug gratefully accepted. The short drive didn't leave much time for conversation, so after exchanging pleasantries, the two sat in silence, while the radio played the local news.

"Sorry I can't take you any further," he told Doug when he dropped him off at the interchange with the secondary road that led to his home, "but my wife's got plans for the afternoon, otherwise, I'd—"

"Don't worry at all," Doug said, "I appreciate the lift, and the walk will do me good."

"Well, it's a nice enough day for sure, and there's a quick stop about a mile up if you need a drink for you and the dog," the custodian said.

"Sure. Great idea," Doug answered. "Thanks again."

The custodian began pulling away, but stopped and rolled down his window for one last word.

"Look, we've all done it," he said.

When Doug raised his eyebrows, the custodian added, "You know, walked off our anger, or stress, or whatever ya wanna call it. Just take it safe, okay?"

"Sure enough. Thanks," Doug answered.

How had the custodian picked up on his angst anyway? He wasn't that transparent, was he?

The quick stop was only a short walk along his route, so once there, Doug tied Thor up outside and went in, returning with a couple of bottled waters, a plastic drink cup for Thor, and two hamburgers—one with the works for himself, and a plain one with no garnishes for Thor.

Just before resuming the trek back to the motel, he switched his smartphone on again. Mara had called. He winced as her voice gave him pangs of guilt for making her worry. He tried to call her back, but only got her voicemail.

"I'm fine. I just had to wrap up a few loose ends in Rhinebeck. Don't worry; I've got a way back. See you this evening. Love you," his message to her said.

There was another call from Della saying that Elzianne LaMonte, along with her complete entourage, had checked out of the hotel two weeks early. She said that this had left management scrambling to fill the rooms and that she had overheard talk of charging the party for the sudden cancellation, and of possibly even hiring a lawyer to pursue recovery of their loss.

"She signed a contract, you know," Della said in her matter-of-fact way.

The rest of the eight mile walk to the motel was uneventful. The custodian had been right about one thing, Doug's stress seemed to melt with each footstep, leaving him with deep feelings of remorse for the harsh way he had talked to Sal.

But, what the heck? Hadn't even Mara lost patience with the old woman recently? And Joe?

Sal/Sylvia had pushed everyone's tolerance. He had just been the first one to be open about it. He stopped berating himself and began to plan how he could do damage control with the woman at the heart of all the turmoil.

What he couldn't figure out yet was how to tell Mara. Keeping a secret this big from his wife felt wrong on many levels, yet was it his place to tell her? Was this the right time? Would waiting allow him some time to work things out and come up with a way to soften the blow, or would waiting serve only to leave his wife with an even deeper sense of betrayal?

He had just about decided to tell her first thing in the morning, when he and Thor arrived at the motel. Wouldn't you just know that the first person he ran into would be Sal, who was out in the parking lot talking on her phone?

Sal clicked her phone off and began to walk towards him. Doug spoke first.

"Look, Sal—Sylvia—"

"Hush, Doug," Sylvia LaMonte told him. "You owe me no apology. I deserved every bit of what you said."

"But it wasn't respectful—" Doug said, before she interrupted him again.

"It was what it was, Doug. The first thing I want to say is that I appreciate that you came to me first with the information that you uncovered. There are some who might have chosen to handle things in, shall we say, a less straightforward manner."

Sylvia LaMonte put her arm through Doug's as he walked with her to the flower-decked boardwalk that lined the river across the street from the motel.

"Well, whatever the case," Doug told her, "It's not like me to be so rude and I want to apologize for my tone and for the accusations and inferences that I made."

Sylvia LaMonte squeezed his arm.

"Please, Doug, let's just forget about it, okay?"

"I was tired . . . worried about how to tell Mara," he persisted.

"Me, too," Sal said. "You know, I want to explain something to you."

"No need," Doug interrupted her.

"Let me finish, Doug," she said gently.

"When the records were unsealed three years ago, I was just as curious as I guess anyone in my position would be. There were so many things I wondered about, but mostly I wondered if my daughter had had a happy life."

Doug looked at her. It sounded strange having Sal refer to Mara as her daughter, yet somehow comforting—as if his initial impression of his wife having been coldly and callously cast off might have been wrong.

"The first thing I did was to try to find her adoptive parents." Sal laughed wryly. "I'm not sure what I was thinking. I didn't know if I might write them, call them, spy on them, you know? I just needed to find them. I hired someone. That's when I learned they were dead. I have to tell you, having that knowledge alone threw me into turmoil."

"How's that?" Doug asked.

"It tore me apart knowing that she had no one," Sal answered. "Then when I learned about Brad dying, I knew I had to find her, so I hired two more people and we did find her—just as she was boarding the ferry for Alaska."

This was just too weird.

"But, that's about when I met her—and when Joe found her. Don't tell me that some cosmic force or something brought us all together or something, Sal," Doug said.

He could feel himself tensing, unsure about just how much more "truth" he could handle.

"Nothing like that," Sylvia LaMonte said, "just coincidence, maybe."

"I don't know, Sal. There's been an awful lot of that—coincidence," Doug said.

"I had left Alaska after Bert's death. I was confused then and not sure what would become of my life. Finding out that Alaska was where she was heading made me want to go to back there and talk to her," Sal continued, "but a little voice told me not to. Anyway, like I just said, I was having my own personal life crisis. I still hadn't come to terms with the death of my husband, Bert, or with the betrayal by my mother and sister, and—well—I returned to Alaska, changed my name to Sal, and began reliving the life that my Bert had taught me to live—a life that had been my only real happiness."

"Wow," Doug mumbled.

"I really tried not to think of Mara for a while. I didn't want her to have to know about me," Sal said. "So I just lived as Sal Kindle. Do you know that Sal stands for Sylvia Anne LaMonte?"

Doug just stared at her and said nothing.

"Now that you know, well, I've already decided to tell her," Sal said. "And I can't stop you from beatin' me to it."

Doug cocked his head. Strange, how Sylvia LaMonte could flip back into her Sal persona so easily. Was that the safe zone in her head, the person called Sal that they all knew?

"And I can't say fer sure jest when it'll happen, ya know?" she continued. "Part of me wants to try ta wait till this mess with Elzianne gets cleared up first, and everything with the bowl and the lawyer and that whole mess gets settled."

They could both see Mara and Joe walking their way. No further discussion could happen right now.

"I'll think of a way to handle my own dilemma," Doug told Sal. "And I promise you, I will do all I can to be mindful of yours in the process."

"I couldn't ask for more than that, Doug," Sal said. "No one could."

Sal turned away briefly as Doug greeted Mara and Joe. Doug could hear her talking on her smartphone. Odd. It would only be a minute later before he understood.

Stepping forward, she began, "Joey? I need to talk to you right away, and Mara, I have something important to talk to you about as well."

All conversation stopped as Sylvia LaMonte spoke with regal authority.

"I've taken the liberty of reserving a booth at a small bistro about five miles from here," she said. "Of all of you, Doug most closely understands what this is about."

Sylvia smiled at Doug, her eyes pleading for him to remain silent.

"Joe and I will meet you both there at five," she continued.

And in a weak attempt at levity she added, "Dinner's on me."

Chapter Fifty-Eight
Rectitude

"What's going on, Sal?" Joe Michael asked his wife when they got back to their room.

Sal jumped right in with what she had to say, not even waiting for Joe to take off his jacket, get them some tea, or behaving in any way like her usual self. She simply sat down and indicated that her husband should do the same.

"With everything that's happened, with all we've been through, it's time for me to come clean—to lay all my cards on the table. If you choose to judge me, or decide you can't understand what I'm about to tell you, then I'll have to accept that. But the bottom line is that I haven't been honest with you, with Doug, or with Mara. Matter of fact, I haven't even been honest with myself," she said.

Joe Michael could feel his blood pressure rise. What now? He looked at his wife sitting there as strong and straightforward in her demeanor as he had ever seen her. Gone was the false bravado that had been the façade of her persona ever since he had first met her. Gone was the vulnerability that made her seem frail and old. In its place was a confident, serious, and determined woman, who was about to come forth with yet another missing piece of the puzzle that her life had become.

"I'm listening, Sylvia," he said, using her given name for the very first time when addressing her, a point that did not go unnoticed by his wife and one made in a manner as equally straightforward as her own.

"The only thing I want to say before we continue, Joe, is that I promise you that this is the last piece of hidden information that I have about myself for you to discover—that, and that I'm sorry it has taken me this long to learn to be open with the you, the man I love more than life itself. I just pray you'll find a way to understand."

"Go on," he said.

"Right before Bert died, I got pregnant."

She paused to look at Joe Michael, but he showed no reaction.

"As a matter of fact, neither of us knew it at the time of his death. I found out about a week after the funeral when I went to the doctor because I couldn't stop vomiting."

"Okay . . ." Joe said softly.

"The doctor said that I might lose the baby, or that I might not," she continued. "So, I took the medicine he gave me, did my best to rest in spite of all the turmoil that was going on, and the short version is that I gave birth to a baby girl six months later."

This time Joe Michael did not remain expressionless. He got up, walked around the room, and then sat back down.

"So, are you trying to tell me that you have a daughter out there somewhere," he said. "Is that the news? Is that what's been making you so distracted for the last several months?"

"Yes, that's what I'm trying to tell you, Joey," she said.

"So what's the deal?" he asked. "It's not like this is news to you or anything. Is she trying to embezzle from you or giving you grief?"

"It's not that simple," Sylvia said. "I made a decision long before the baby was born that I was in no position—financially or emotionally—to raise a child. I consulted with several agencies and finally settled on one that would allow me to give birth to the child and turn it over within twenty-four hours to the adoptive parents. "

"Wow," Joe said. "So you lost your husband and then gave up his baby right after? Wow, Sylvia. That's a tough one to understand. Real tough."

Sylvia said nothing, instead lowering her head as her husband stood again and paced the room.

"Do you know what I'd give to have my children back again?" he said, his voice low and gravelly. "I'd give my own life if that's what it took, and you—you just handed your newborn daughter over to a pair of strangers and simply walked away. Amazing."

"I was afraid you might not understand," she said meekly. "I was under so much pressure. I literally did not know where my next meal was coming from. I was lost. I did what I thought was right. The agency even let me help screen the applicants. I could see the interviews through one-way glass. I knew the right ones the minute I saw them.

"I even named the baby. I called her Jane. They let me hold her for as long as I wanted to that first day—just to make sure. When it came time to hand her over to the nurse, I almost changed my mind, but I knew that she'd be in better hands and have a loving and stable life, so I gave her to the nurse, signed the papers, and never looked back."

Sylvia LaMonte dabbed tears from her eyes.

"Every year on her birthday, the adoptive parents would send me an update through the agency, but no pictures. They had some policy about pictures. The records were sealed, too, and I learned that they would not be able to be unsealed for thirty-five years.

"Even then, I didn't try to find them, that is—"

Sylvia LaMonte got up and blew her nose before sitting back down.

"That is, before they found me."

"What do you mean they found you?" Joe asked her.

"About three years ago, the records were unsealed and the agency sent me a notice. Along with it, they sent me the additional information that my daughter's adoptive parents had been killed in an accident. They also told me that she had completed college, gotten married, and that there would be no further communication."

"Okay," Joe said.

"I decided to find her," Sylvia said. "My plan was to know about her, but not approach her. Then, somehow, I learned that her husband had died and that she was heading up to Alaska. By then, I was living in Spokane, but I decided to go find her. Then I changed my mind. What right did I have to disrupt her life? So, I headed back to Alaska intending to stay alone, took on my identity as Sal, and tried to resume the life that Bert and I had lived."

"So, are you saying that she's in Alaska?" Joe asked.

"Yes. I've know about her for some time now, but she doesn't know about me."

"So, what's different now, Sal?" Joe asked, getting up and putting his arm around his trembling wife.

"Someone else knows now," Sal said. "Her current husband."

"How do you know this?" Joe asked.

"Because—because—" Sylvia LaMonte crumbled into her husband's comforting arms, speaking through the sobs that wracked her body. "I never planned to tell her. Why disrupt her life? But now I have no choice. I don't know how—I don't know if I can . . ."

Joe Michael got up and got a cool cloth to wipe away the tears from his wife's face.

"I'm not sure you'll be able to handle this, Joey," Sal blurted. "I'm so scared."

"Look, Sal," Joe Michael said. "Whatever it is, I'll handle it, okay. Just tell me. Tell me so we can face this together. "

"Sylvia LaMonte stopped crying and looked her husband squarely in the eye. "It's Mara, Joe. Mara is my daughter."

"Mara? Mara's your daughter!" Joe said, stunned. "I'm gonna need a minute to absorb this."

"It's not like you think, Joey," Sal said. "I didn't mean to follow her so closely. It's just that everything fell into place the way it did from the first minute we met. It started with me being able to help her kind of anonymously, but then it became more. Still, I never planned to tell her. There was no reason to shake up her life. Then when Doug found the papers . . ."

"What papers?" Joe asked.

"The adoption papers . . . last week with the rest of the information he turned up on the Kindle and LaMonte families. He put it together, and yesterday he showed them to me. That's what the meeting is for this afternoon. I plan to tell her. I have to, Joey. I can't expect Doug to do it or to keep a secret like this from his wife. I only hope she won't hate me."

For a long time, neither of them said anything. Sal went into the bathroom to freshen up and Joe paced the room. His army buddy had never told him that his daughter was adopted. It wouldn't have mattered even if he had known. He still would have watched out for her. How horrible this must have been for Sal—to keep such a secret for so long.

Something had told him to give the feather to Mara. Maybe there was some kind of destiny thing at play here after all. Whatever the case, his decision was immediate, and surprisingly easy to make.

"Mara's always been like a daughter to me ever since I promised her father I'd look after her," he told his wife when she came back into the room. "And you, Sal, you are my wife and I love you. We said we'd tackle everything together, and that's how we'll handle this. Together. I'm not sure how, but we'll handle it and whatever we do will be right."

Sylvia LaMonte ran to her husband's arms. Never in her life had she believed that she would find someone such as he. "I love you, Joey," she said simply. "And I always will."

Chapter Fifty-Nine
Jane, Understood

The booth that Sal had reserved was along a far wall and like the others in the small bistro, built with tall backs that provided a great deal of privacy. Mara and Doug were already inside when Sal and Joe arrived at the restaurant. As each of them sipped their wine, their conversation was light, if not somewhat guarded.

After several minutes of light banter, Sal began.

"I'd like to thank you for coming here with me tonight, while knowing that something different than our usual time together would be coming forth. Before I begin, I want to thank each of you for coming into my life and tell you that I love you."

After the toast, Mara leaned over to Doug to ask if he knew what was coming down.

"Sal's scaring me," she said. "Is it bad news—like is she dying or something?"

Doug squeezed her hand and looked Sal's way, nodding for her to continue.

"I know that each of you has noticed a change in me, beginning way back when you came looking for me out on the water on that foggy April day in Juneau," she said.

No one else spoke. Mara smiled uncomfortably, while Joe shifted in his chair.

"I also know that I dropped a bombshell on everyone when you learned that my given name was Sylvia LaMonte, and that I was born into a wealthy family outside of Alaska."

Sylvia sipped her wine and looked directly at each of them, one by one, before continuing.

"Recently—within the past week—well—"

Sylvia LaMonte pause, her discomfort palpable.

"Maybe I can help, Sal," Doug said, standing.

"I should . . ." she protested weakly.

"If not for me, for the discovery that I made," Doug began, "we wouldn't be having this conversation."

He stopped to sip his wine, looking at each of them as he did. Joe Michael had put his hand over his wife's, while Mara sat frozen with an expression of dread on her face.

"Last week, when Joe and I went to Albany to research the Kindle and LaMonte families, we found plenty of information to support us in reclaiming the Edo period bowl from Elzianne. As you know, all of that has been forwarded to Dennis Connor Sr. He is currently preparing our case, and it looks like it'll be a strong one."

This was proving to be more difficult than Doug had imagined.

"Look," he said, "no sense beating around the bush anymore. I found something when I was in Albany looking through the records, okay?"

"Okay, Doug," Mara said.

"Mara," he said, speaking directly to his wife. "I don't even know how to tell you this. I just want you to know that the last few days have been hell for me—wondering if you should know, then wondering how you should know . . ."

"Just tell me, Doug," Mara told him.

Sylvia LaMonte stood up.

"Doug uncovered some information that had been sealed for thirty-five years," she said. "Information that I had hoped would remain undiscovered. It's not that I'm ashamed of it, I want you all to know that—especially you, Mara, but information that would serve no useful purpose for you to know. Information that it has been my greatest fear would one day surface to cause you pain."

"Doug, what's going on?" Mara said, looking shaken.

"I was never a great believer in destiny—you know, in that way that some people think that their life has been predetermined. When I first met you, Mara, it was purely unintentional. I call it happenstance, and I thought nothing of it at the time. The fact that I kept running into you when you needed me amused me, and made me feel important. I liked you right away. That's why I called you Jane. The name, Jane, has always had a special importance to me."

Mara sat quietly, listening as Sal spoke.

"When Doug discovered the paperwork in Albany, the news of its existence came as no real surprise. I had discovered it myself about three years earlier, and had decided to take the information it contained with me to my grave. I saw no need to bring it forward. I felt that doing so would cause more harm than good. I want you all to know that.

"But when Doug came to me with the information, after having stumbled upon it himself, I knew that I could no longer keep the secret hidden."

Sylvia LaMonte dabbed her eyes.

"Joe knows about this. I told him this morning. And of course, Doug has known since last week. The reason we're here now is to tell you, Mara. To tell you here with those who love you and who want you to know that we will always be here whenever you need us."

Mara reached into her pocket for a Kleenex and felt the feather deep inside. What else could there be that hadn't happened to her already? She took a deep breath and braced herself for the news.

"Maybe it would be best if you just read it here first, Mara," Doug said, handing her the folded papers that he had been carrying around for a week.

She took them from him and began to read, stopping when she got to the adoption papers that listed her parents names.

"I need you all to know that I've always known that I was adopted," she said. "My mother told me when I was old enough to understand. She told me the whole story about my birth mother having to give me up and prepared me for the fact that I would never know her. I was okay with that. My parents loved me and I loved them. It didn't matter to me that someone had given me up to a good home. As I became an adult, I knew that that meant love— that someone had cared enough to see that I had what maybe they couldn't give me. My mother taught me to be okay with that—to feel compassion and acceptance."

Doug put his arm around her. "Keep reading."

Mara did as instructed and re-read the papers.

"It looks like my original name was Jane," she said.

Then she put it together.

"It says that a woman named Sylvia LaMonte Kindle was . . ."

Suddenly she felt faint. How could this be happening? As much as she wanted to run, she felt frozen in time—unable to move.

"I'm your birth mother, Mara," Sylvia LaMonte said simply.

Mara gasped, her eyes darting between Sal and Doug, then to Joe.

"What your mother told you about me was true, and what I want you to know is that I helped choose her from the many who wanted to take you home. You were a beautiful baby—quiet and serene. Your mother had that same quality, that same beauty and serenity. I knew the minute I saw her that she was the one."

"You two met?" Mara asked.

"Not really," Sal answered, explaining the one-way glass and the process as it was in those days. "I almost backed out at the last minute, but I knew I wouldn't be a fit mother for you—not with everything that was going on. You were what we called a change-of-life baby—unplanned, unexpected, and a secret even from your father, who died before knowing that I was pregnant."

Mara looked at Sylvia LaMonte as if seeing her for the first time. Somehow, she managed to speak even though her mind was jumbled and racing in a panic of random thoughts.

"I guess you know that I'm pretty shocked," she managed to spit out. "And that I'm going to need some time to absorb all of this."

"I don't expect you to treat me any differently," Sal said. "Your mother is the person who raised you and who loved you during your entire life. I would never want to take that from you even in a small way."

Mara looked at the old woman and said nothing. She was at a complete loss for words. Doug squeezed her shoulders with one arm and drew her near, while Joe Michael clasped the hand of his wife.

"I'm not really that hungry," Mara finally said.

"I understand," Sylvia answered.

"I'm not mad at you," Mara told her. "I just need some time."

Chapter Sixty
Healing and Bonding

A strange calm embraced the soul of Sylvia LaMonte. It was as if the greatest burden of her life had been lifted from her heart. Mara would come around. She felt certain of that, and she planned to ask nothing of her because of the revelation. It was enough for her that she had reclaimed her own life. Although she would strive to remain a part of Mara's, she would let Mara settle in her own place of inner peace.

"It's weird," Joe Michael told her, as the two of them remained behind and ordered a second glass of wine.

"What's that, Joey?"

"All of it. Just weird. Kinda thought she'd have trouble with it. She seemed pretty calm."

In a way, though, he understood. Having been through enough loss and discovered enough shocking truth about his own life, he, too, had become almost numb.

"I think it went as well as we could hope," he told his wife. "Now we'll just have to see."

"Yes. We'll just have to see," Sylvia said. "I want to go home soon, Joey."

"Me, too," he said.

"I want to sit in my chair by the window and watch the fog come over the water."

"And I want to sit there with you," Joe laughed. "Only maybe now I'll make tea sometimes. You know, since you've been through so much."

"If only this were the end of it," Sylvia laughed, "But we still have to face Elzianne and that whole mess."

"Yup," he answered.

"Part of me feels like just letting it go. You know, not even fighting her," Sylvia said.

"Look, Sal, I don't blame you for feeling tired, but I'm not going to let you be a quitter either. The woman's wrong and she needs to be dealt with. The whole thing makes me so mad, I sometimes figure a gun would take care of her and that would be that."

"Don't talk that way, Joe, you know you don't mean that," Sylvia admonished him.

"I know, Sal," Joe said. "Let's go back to the room. We'll just pay for the wine and leave it."

As they made their way out of the dimly lit restaurant, neither of them saw the shadowy figure in the next booth watching their every move.

Not until they reached the edge of the parking lot did she make her move.

"Stop right there, dear sister," Elzianne LaMonte demanded, raising the derringer she had just pulled from her purse.

Sylvia LaMonte and Joe Michael turned around slowly.

"I loved your gun idea," Elzianne said to Joe. "Imitation *is* the sincerest form of flattery, don't you agree?"

"You'd be the expert on that, wouldn't you, Elzianne?" Sylvia answered without revealing the intense fear she felt for her safety.

"Tell your eskimo to give me the papers," Elzianne hissed.

"Tell me yourself," Joe Michael said.

"The proper term is *Native elder*," Mara said, stepping out from behind one of the parked cars. "And by the way, just so you know—"

Thor lunged at almost the exact moment that Elzianne spun around, knocking the gun from her hand and causing her to fall backwards onto the ground. The fall didn't stop Elzianne from scrambling for her gun, but Mara kicked it out of her reach.

"My mother was right about you. You are the face of evil," Mara said.

Two police cars pulled up as a small crowd gathered around the scene.

"I saw the whole thing," one of the servers who worked at the restaurant told an officer. "And on top of pulling a gun on this nice old couple, she left without paying her bill," he said, pointing to Elzianne.

"We're gonna need a medic," another officer said. "I think she might've broken a hip."

Mara ran to Sal and Joe, hustling them away from the scene and back inside the restaurant. A third officer followed them inside. Moments later, Doug arrived, where he found them all sitting in one of the tall booths.

"What's going on," he said, visibly upset.

"Where's Thor?" Mara asked.

"In the car," Doug answered. "Now what's going on?"

"Excuse me, sir," the officer said, standing.

"He's with us," Joe Michael said.

"Step back," the officer told Doug. "I don't want to have to arrest you for interfering with police business."

Doug did as instructed and went outside to check on Thor. As he walked among the people still standing outside the restaurant, he pieced together the story of what had happened. Meanwhile, back inside, the officer continued taking statements, beginning with Sal.

"My name is Sylvia LaMonte Michael," she began. "And the woman on the ground is my only sister, Elzianne LaMonte."

Sal went on to explain how she and Joe and just exited the restaurant when Elzianne had confronted them with the gun.

"There's a long history of animosity between us," Sal said, "and we are currently involved in legal action against her. If it hadn't been for my daughter showing up . . ."

Just then, Sal collapsed against her husband's shoulder as she began to sob.

Thirty minutes later, the scene at the restaurant became normal once more and a shaken Sylvia LaMonte emerged from the restaurant with her husband and the daughter she had given up thirty-eight years ago.

"I heard what happened," Doug said. "They took Elzianne to the hospital, but the police assured me that she'll be placed under arrest as soon as she's been treated. They took the derringer into custody and got statements from a half dozen witnesses. As far as I know, everyone said the same thing.

"You okay, Mara?" he asked his wife.

"More than okay," Mara answered, smiling at Sal and at Joe. "I mean, we're all a little shaken for sure, but we're family—literally," she said, smiling at Sal, "and we'll get each other through it."

Doug stood there speechless.

"It's been a roller coaster of a day," Sylvia LaMonte told him. "For all of us."

"I'm gonna get her back to the room for some rest," Joe Michael said. "I'm thinking it might be a good idea if we all rested after all this."

"You're right, Joe," Doug said.

Mara walked up to Sylvia LaMonte as the two embraced and as their husbands watched years of estrangement melt away. On the ground beside Mara, the feather had fallen to the ground. Doug picked it up and placed it in his own pocket with ultimate care. He'd return it to his wife once they were back in their room. Meanwhile, he would be right there beside her.

Chapter Sixty-One
Is Peace Overrated?

"I can't really explain this, Joey," Sylvia LaMonte said as she lay next to her husband for a nap, "but some part of me thinks I should visit Elzianne—and believe me when I say that I am as surprised as you are to hear myself say this."

"Can we talk about this later?" Joe answered. "I don't think right now that it would be a good . . ."

Joe Michael fell into a deep sleep, leaving his wife beside him still awake. When he awoke and found her gone, he somehow knew she was with Elzianne.

Since no charges had yet been filed against Elzianne, Sylvia was able to get in to visit her despite a police presence at the door.

"I appreciate you letting me in, Lou," she said to the childhood friend, who was now a retired member of the New York State Police, and who had taken a postretirement job with the local police force to guard prisoners.

Lou took her purse and searched her before letting her enter. He also summoned a nurse into in the room.

Elzianne was half asleep when her sister walked up to her bed, but her eyes flew open at the sight as she became agitated and tried to sit up.

"Did you come back to finish me off?" she snarled.

"You sound afraid, Elzi," Sylvia LaMonte said evenly. "Perhaps you're projecting your own inclinations onto me."

"Nurse!" Elzi hollered.

The nurse approached Elzianne and reminded her that she could push a button to control her pain with her IV line.

Elzianne gave the button a series of punches.

"Now, Ms. LaMonte, remember, it will only let you have so much at a time," the nurse told her.

"I'll sit with her," Sylvia said, smiling.

"She's been agitated since she arrived," the nurse said.

"I won't stay long," Sylvia replied.

"I'm not sure why I'm here, either," Sylvia continued, turning to face Elzianne. "I think I'm going soft in my old age. I just wanted to see if maybe somehow, some way, I've been wrong about you. If maybe there had been some misunderstanding . . ."

Elzianne's eyes fluttered closed, then open again, as if she'd gotten her second wind.

"You were always so naïve, Sylvia. So—so easy," Elzi began. "I could never understand why you just always rolled over and let everyone walk all over you."

"Nice matters, Elzi," Sylvia said rather defensively.

"Haven't you ever heard that good guys come in last?" Elzi chuckled. "Now here you are again, staring right down the throat of your own personal dragon."

"I guess I was wrong in trying to give you the benefit of the doubt," Sylvia said. "Somehow I thought that age would have mellowed you—matured you. If anything, it's only empowered you to nurture your bitterness and hate."

"Come on, Sylvia. Do you think that all that righteous talk is going to change anything? That maybe I'll cry and beg your forgiveness?"

Elzianne LaMonte straightened her sheets and punched the IV line dose button again.

"I'll make a deal with you, sister, you give up your claim to the Edo bowl— you know, say it was all a misunderstanding—and maybe I'll decide to let you live out the rest of your life without bothering you or your family again."

Sylvia LaMonte walked away and didn't look back. She had done all she could to bridge the gap that had estranged them. It was obvious that Elzianne would never change. The realization enveloped her with a peace that had eluded her for much of her adult life.

"Feel better soon," she called back.

How easy it was to be kind to the sister who had spent a lifetime trying to control her, now that she no longer blamed herself for the estrangement.

"Thank you, Lou," she told her friend. "I know you might have bent the rules a bit for me, but I want you to know that this visit meant more to me than you'll ever know."

"I'm back, Joe," she called as she entered their room. "It's such a beautiful day. Let's go for a walk."

Chapter Sixty-Two
Starting to Wrap Things Up

Doug was on the phone with Dennis Connor when Joe and Sal returned from their walk. He continued talking while they took off their coats. Mara had her ear near his, trying to hear what was being said.

"Well," Doug said after sitting down. "There's plenty of news."

Authentication experts hired by Dennis Connor's firm had confirmed that the bowl Mara used for Thor's watering bowl was indeed an Edo Period Japanese bowl and one of only two that were ever made. The other was in the possession of the British monarchy. Because of the unique dip in the glaze on this piece, it was deemed to be more valuable than its counterpart.

"Wow!" Mara gasped. "Thank goodness Thor has a gentle mouth."

The digital photos and chronographs that Dennis Jr. had used to catalog the tsunami debris, although deemed to be overkill initially, had turned out to have provided definite proof that the bowl was recovered by Beachmoppers, Inc. and also that it was used as Thor's water bowl, where it sat beside the bench outside the gift shop that clearly showed the name Beachmoppers above it.

"Dennis even has a photo of Thor drinking from the bowl and Mara leaning over beside him pulling weeds," Doug said.

"Maybe we can go home soon," Sal said. "It sounded like we might be able to," Doug answered. "Apparently Dennis Connor has already discussed his findings with the New York Cultural Museum, who will release ownership of the bowl back to Beachmoppers at the end of the exhibit, which is next week. He said that they have amended their advertising to state that it is on loan from Beachmoppers, Inc. and by mutual agreement with us—via Dennis Connor—will drop any claim to the bowl."

"Sounds good unless the media get ahold of it," Joe Michael said.

Doug proceeded to explain that the museum curator, the museum board, and Beachmoppers (as represented by his firm) would issue a joint statement to the effect that previously unknown and rightful owners have come forward, that the museum respects the veracity of their claim, and that the museum wishes to return the item to its rightful owners, while being ultimately grateful for the opportunity to have displayed such a priceless work of art.

The article would also express the intent of both the museum and of Beachmoppers to return the item to the people of Japan, who had suffered the loss of this priceless item that miraculously made its way across the ocean to Alaska and then to New York after the tsunami.

"It sounds like things are finally wrapping up," Sal said.

"Well, there's still Elzianne," Joe said.

No one said anything in response. Joe Michael was right, though, there was still Elzianne.

Chapter Sixty-Three
OMG!

Dennis Connor assured them that the trial for Elzianne LaMonte was not likely to occur for at least six months, but since they had already received a confession—although no expression of remorse—from Elzianne, and had the testimony of Julia Bruce, her daughter, and several others who had peripheral knowledge of what was going on, including Mara, Sal, and others, there was little likelihood that she would escape conviction.

"We'll need the formality of your testimony," Dennis Connor said, "but nothing will happen anytime soon, I assure you."

"But what about Julia Bruce?" Mara asked. "She's dying."

"We've taken a sworn affidavit via both written and video testimony," he answered. "If she dies, it will definitely weaken the case from the perspective of her testimony, but I believe that the evidence against Elzianne is so overwhelming that we can still get a conviction even without the testimony of Julia Bruce."

"I hate the thought of having to come back," Sylvia LaMonte said after hearing Doug's recounting of his conversation with their attorney, "but maybe we could work things so that the memorial to Monsignor St. Jean can be dedicated then, so we need to come back only once."

"Yes, that would be ideal," Doug agreed. "Anyway, that was pretty much the nuts and bolts of what I learned."

Since there was little else to do, the four of them went into Rhinebeck, stopping at St. Aloysius to discuss a site for the memorial to Monsignor St. Jean.

Joe and Sal were inside the church hall talking with the custodian, when Mara and Doug walked in, followed by Sal's retired NYSP friend, Lou, and two Rhinebeck police officers.

"There's been a shooting," Lou began. "At the hospital."

Everyone stopped talking as Lou approached Sal.

"There are two—this is harder than I thought it—I'm sorry, Sylvia, but your sister, Elzianne, is dead."

"My word," Sylvia said, surprised that she felt any emotion at all.

"You said there were two victims?" Doug said, stepping forward.

"They're waiting to notify next of kin, but it looks like the other victim is Julia Bruce," Lou told them.

Mara sat down. "I can't believe it," she murmured.

"What happened?" Joe Michael said, approaching the officers and facing them directly.

"It's pretty straightforward—and this has been corroborated by multiple witnesses," Lou told them.

"Apparently, Julia Bruce came to visit Ms. LaMonte, claiming that she was her personal assistant," Lou began. "I wasn't on duty, but the officer that was apparently was convinced enough to let her in. He said that Ms. LaMonte even greeted Ms. Bruce and said something to the effect that it was about time she came back."

Sal, Joe Michael, Doug, and Mara exchanged glances.

"According to the officer on duty," Lou continued, "he had no reason to suspect anything about the visit. Ms. Bruce was dressed impeccably, carried an armful of papers, and behaved in a professional manner."

"Apparently, seconds after setting the papers on the nightstand in front of Ms. LaMonte, Ms. Bruce pulled a gun out from under her coat and shot Ms. LaMonte point blank in the head," one of the city police officers told them. "Then, before anyone had a chance to react, she placed the gun to her own head and pulled the trigger."

"This is unbelievable," Mara gasped. "Julia Bruce was dying . . ."

"There was a note found in the apartment of Ms. Bruce," Lou said. "In it, she expressed her love for her only daughter, and talked about how the doctors had said that the cancer had spread to her brain and that she only had a week or so to live.

"She went on to elaborate, talking about how she was of sound mind and body considering her death sentence, and that while she still had her mind, she wanted to make sure that Elzianne LaMonte never hurt anyone again. 'My life doesn't matter anymore,' she had written, 'except in that I have this one last opportunity to right some of the so many wrongs that Elzianne LaMonte has spread among all who knew her.'"

"What about her daughter?" Mara asked.

"Her daughter confirmed what the note had said about Ms. Bruce having only a week left to live. She said that in the last twenty-four hours that her mother had seemed more like her old self than she had in months. From what I've seen of cancer patients, that is as clear a sign as one could receive that she would be gone within a day."

"Will you need anything from us?" Doug asked. "No," the third officer replied. "We simply wanted to notify Mrs. Michael and express our condolences to the family."

"Thank you, officers," Sylvia LaMonte said, escorting them to the door. "I'll see that some kind of arrangements are made as soon as you tell me to proceed."

Chapter Sixty-Four
Holdings

Elzianne LaMonte was cremated the next day, after forensics experts had finished gathering any evidence they might need. The case was labeled murder by probable medically provoked dementia and suicide. The case was closed at the request of the district attorney, after a lengthy discussion with Sylvia LaMonte and with Julia Bruce's daughter, Carol.

Sylvia organized a simple memorial at the LaMonte homestead, also releasing a modest obituary that documented Elzianne's existence on this earth. About twenty people attended—mostly childhood friends, who had never left Rhinebeck, each of whom stood in silent reverence while Elzianne's ashes were scattered into the Hudson River.

"It's more than she deserved," Joe Michael told his wife.

"She can't hurt us anymore, Joey," Sylvia LaMonte said.

When the ceremony was over, Sylvia LaMonte walked away from her sister one last time. "I wish I could say I miss her, but when I look deep inside, there's nothing there," she told Mara later. "Absolutely nothing but the sad knowledge of what might have been between sisters who actually cared about each other."

"I'm sorry you never had her," Mara said. "But from everything I have learned, it wasn't your fault that you didn't."

Sal looked at the daughter she had given up at birth. What a fine woman she had turned out to be—a beautiful combination of both kindness and caring. She couldn't take any credit for that. Mara's real parents had taught her those traits. But God had blessed Sylvia LaMonte, and guided her in making the right decision about the baby she had called Jane.

Now he had blessed her again by not only letting her meet the woman she had become, but by bringing her daughter back fully into her life. She wasn't sure she deserved it; then, again, why not? Hadn't she done her best in life within the circumstances she had been dealt? She crossed *be kind to yourself* off her mental bucket list and let herself feel the joy she had come to know.

A smile crossed her face as she watched Mara and Doug walk ahead of her, hand in hand. Dennis Connor had told her that she would be inheriting Elzianne's entire estate. Even after restitution and fines and bills, he had told her, it still amounted to three quarters of a billion dollars.

Yet the news hadn't brought her real joy. True, it had been a relief to know that the *Driftfeather* and the *Storm Roamer* were free and clear again—also Beachmoppers and their landing craft. But Sylvia LaMonte had long ago learned that money could bring as much evil as it could joy, and so she had learned to appreciate relationships more than dollars.

The biggest satisfaction would be in knowing that Doug and Mara would never have to worry again. She and Joe had already left half of their estate to them before learning the truth about Mara. The rest they had left to Joe's niece, Della. Della would be comfortable for the rest of her life, but Doug and Mara would now be heirs to the complete LaMonte estate, including the property in Rhinebeck and other area real estate holdings. Together, Sal and Joe decided to tell Doug and Mara later, after they returned to Hoonah. For now, they had just let the two know that the *Driftfeather* and *Storm Roamer* were still theirs, and that alone had given them more relief than they could have imagined.

Sylvia and Joe had also decided that they would set up a generous trust for Julia Bruce's daughter, Carol, whose mother had loved her so much and whose joy she would no longer know. Both Carol and Julia had helped them and the trust was easy enough for them to implement, so that Carol and her family would never have to worry about money again. Dennis Connor would notify Carol in writing. There was no need to expect gratitude or look for validation from her. The giving in itself had provided all they needed.

Thor bounded up to them as they later walked past a small antique shop from which Sylvia LaMonte returned with a beautiful cut-crystal bowl.

"I know this isn't the Edo porcelain that you used to drink from," she told him, "but I think you'll find it satisfactory."

Joe Michael laughed at the gesture. "Sometimes I think you love that dog more than you do me."

"And sometimes I just think you think too much, Joe Michael," Sal laughed, putting her arm through his.

"A few more days and we should be headed home," he told her.

"I can't think of anything I'm looking forward to more than being there," Sal said. "But first there's some loose ends to wrap up with the estate. For one thing, I'm going to have to hire a caretaker for the house. We'll probably have to fly back in a few months to sort through everything, and I was thinking that—"

Joe Michael pulled her close. "And you say that I'm the one who thinks too much."

Chapter Sixty-Five
Packing Up

Joe Michael threw a duffel bag towards Doug, who caught it and lifted it into the Cessna. After two months in New York and a lifetime of drama, it felt good to be heading back to Hoonah again.

When he bent down to pick up another bag, he saw the feather he had returned to Mara lying on the ground. She would never have left it there if she had known. He knew that for sure.

"Are you missing something important?" he called to Mara. "Something like the feather, maybe?"

She didn't answer.

"I'm sure glad I had the idea to return it to you when I did," he said. "Something told me that it was time and it looks like something was right. Anyway, it must have fallen out of your pocket because I found it on the ground this morning."

"Did you say something, Joe?" Mara said, sticking her head out the door of the plane where she had been clear back inside the tail helping stack their luggage as Doug lifted it up to her.

"Doug, have you seen Thor's blanket?"

"I don't think she heard you, Joe," Doug said.

Joe Michael stuck the feather back into his pocket. He'd talk to Mara about the feather later, when there was more time—maybe during a quiet walk or something. She'd have to be more careful about losing it. He knew she'd agree, even if it was starting to get a bit raggedy from all the use.

It was weird how the feather kept coming back to him though, even when he tried to share it with others. He could hardly remember a time when it wasn't jabbing him or sticking up out of his pocket. A couple of times he could have sworn he saw the red dot move, but at his age, his eyes were always playing tricks on him.

Maybe he'd listen to Sal and get his cataracts removed this winter. She said it was a simple procedure. What the heck! Glasses were a pain anyway, especially in the rainy and windy weather that was the norm in Southeast Alaska.

Sylvia LaMonte Kindle walked up to her husband and tucked her arm inside his.

"The ceremony was beautiful, wasn't it?"

"It really was," Joe answered. "It's the first consulate I've ever visited."

"The ambassador to Japan was so grateful to us for having the ceremony in New York City. He assured me that the people of Japan were more than honored to receive the rare porcelain bowl, especially in view of the devastation wrought by the tsunami.

"Apparently no one on either continent can believe that it survived the earthquake and tsunami, not to mention got all the way to Alaska without sustaining damage."

"And it survived being stolen by your sister, Elzianne, too," Doug said, as he walked by.

"Well, she'll not be stealing it or anything else again," Sylvia replied. "Although it wouldn't surprise me if she didn't figure out a way to carry out her mission of evil from the beyond."

"Whatever the case," Joe Michael said, "she's been exposed for who and what she was. I don't think she can hurt us anymore, but I don't blame you for feeling wary. When someone's done the things that she's done to you, you can't help but feel guarded."

"Hell's bells, if ya think I'm gonna let that shrew rule me from her place in the hot seat, then ya ain't seen the soul a Sal Kindle Michael, husband," Sylvia said reverting to her Sal way of speaking.

"This is going to be an interesting final chapter in my life," Joe laughed, placing his arm around his wife's shoulders and squeezing her close. "Most men are lucky to keep one wife into their old age, but I've got me two—all wrapped up in one beautiful package."

"We're just about ready to board," Doug called. "C'mere, Thor."

Thor ran to Doug and tried to climb into the plane but couldn't quite manage, so Doug lifted him inside and latched him in his cage.

"Everyone take care of whatever you have to take care of and be belted into the plane in fifteen minutes, okay?"

On their way back to the plane from the restrooms, Joe gave the feather back to Mara.

"You must have dropped it," he said. "I found it on the ground this morning. That's what I was trying to tell you when you were packing the plane."

"Thank God you found it, Joe! I can't believe I almost lost it again. Just the other day Doug said he had found it and had given it back to me, too. I definitely need to be more mindful of this feather."

Joe Michael chuckled at her reaction. He had been right about what the feather meant to her.

"Don't you know by now that neither of us is ever going to be able to shake this feather loose," he laughed. "Kinda makes you feel like a bird or something, doesn't it?"

"As if that would be a bad thing, huh?" Mara answered.

Doug helped them into the plane, having already seated Sal in one of the rear seats.

He checked her seatbelt again and then latched Joe's around him as well, before helping Mara into the plane and also securing her restraint.

For the next several days, they flew by day and slept by night, taking only a minimal amount of clothing and personal items with which to freshen up each day. Each time, before departure, Doug would strap them in securely again, before lifting off.

Thor loved the travel, and especially loved the long walks he got to go on as the small party checked out each of their stops along the way.

Their last stop in Whitehorse had gone without incident, with none of the hassles from customs that they had experienced on the way south. Doug, more than any of them, had been relieved. Could this be the first sign that their troubles were now over and that life could be lived as it should be—free from the constant surprises and angst that had marked the past few years?

When they lifted off from Whitehorse it had been late afternoon, and he had done so knowing that the trip would be short enough to get them safely home before dark. He squeezed Mara's hand as they flew along and she squeezed his back—a silent acknowledgment that all was well and that they were going home.

The sky was so blue, and a stream of orange-soaked clouds filtered the sun. Mara touched the feather in her pocket, savoring its comfortable presence. Joe was right. The feather was as much a part of her—of them—as were their heartbeats. She found herself touching it more now that she had almost lost it, as if trying to undo the mistake of letting it out of her grasp.

When they got home, she would find a way to secure it, but then, was that even a good idea? Didn't it need to be free from any tether in order to do its job? She tucked it deeper into her pocket, then, as if to distract herself from any more thoughts about the feather, pulled out the maps to help follow their route home.

"I don't think we need those," Doug said.

"I know, but I figure it will help me learn," she answered.

Doug smiled.

"Maybe so," he said.

Last Chapter
Heading Home

After studying the maps, Mara folded them back up. When she turned around to put them into the sleeve behind her seat, she could see both Sal and Joe asleep in the rear seats of the Cessna. She smiled at the sight of Joe's hand resting on Sal's lap and Sal's hand resting on top of his. Reaching back, she pulled a comforter up over their legs, and then turned back around to enjoy the sights of the beautiful, clear fall day.

In an hour or so they would be back in Hoonah, another chapter of their life closed. It was true, wasn't it, that something good always came from something bad? In a surprise move, Sal and Joe had presented them with the deed to both Beachmoppers and the landing craft, and that deed had been dated long before Mara had come to know the truth about the old woman, who had mysteriously appeared in her life one day when she needed her most.

"We're also leaving most of our bank account, the house, and the cabin to Della," Sal had told them. "It's not that we want to be morbid, but we're old now and all that's really important to us is each other—and the love of those close to us, so we had Dennis Connor draw up a will before we left."

The rest of the news about their inheritance would be part of their homecoming celebration—at least that is what Sal and Joe had whispered to each other earlier that day.

Mara and Doug had enjoyed the celebration held by the Japanese consulate in New York earlier that week, during which Sal had returned the Edo period rare porcelain bowl to the people of Japan, shocking even hardened news reporters when they donated the substantial reward to the continued tsunami relief in that country.

"Tell Thor not to worry, though," Sal had told Mara, "I bought him a crystal bowl in New York."

"I'm going to cook us a big dinner this Sunday," Mara said to Doug, as she closed her eyes and nestled comfortably in her seat. "You know, to celebrate how everything turned out."

The steady drone of the engine was hypnotic, making her snuggle more deeply into her seat. It was warm, comfortable, and so relaxing that she almost forgot she was in the plane, instead thinking that she was home in bed.

What was that thump?

Why was Doug suddenly slumping over in his seat?

"Doug. Doug!" she shook him hard, which only made him slump over even more, his seatbelt the only thing holding him up.

Her scream was long and shrill, and totally within her racing mind, as her body reacted with the speed of time standing still. Before any sound could reach her lips, she reached over and undid his seatbelt, letting her husband slump into the narrow space between their seats. There was no time to try to move him or to slide into the seat to try to control the Cessna before she saw the left wing crumble in slow motion against the jagged mountainside.

She felt herself tumbling, feeling her back slam against the ceiling of the plane, where for just the flash of an instant she could see Sal and Joe below her, their bodies slumped together. Three times she tumbled past them, once seeing Doug fly past her inside the tiny confines of the airplane.

Then there was a thud, a long spinning slide, and then silence—the final noise being the sound of one of the plane's doors falling to the ground. She was on the ceiling and Doug was there beside her. She felt for his pulse. There was none. She tried to roll him over to help him breathe, but the pain in her ribs kept her from accomplishing the task, even as she tried with all her might to overcome it.

Why wasn't he moving? Coming to? She reached for his pulse again, and felt the warmth of blood creeping under his arm. With a mighty push, she pulled him over, falling back with her own pain as she did. If she could just stop the bleeding . . .

"Sal! Joe!" she screamed, this time out loud. "Help me! Help me!"

There was nothing but silence.

"Sal! Wake up! Joe! Joe!"

When she finally saw them, she knew why they couldn't answer. Fighting the urge to faint, she reached again for Doug, placing her mouth firmly over his and willing him to breathe. Only the whimper behind her made her look up as she felt Thor tugging on her pant leg.

"No, Thor. Stop! Drop It! Let go!"

She tried to swat at him, but he kept pulling. She could see his crate lying in the snow outside the plane, its door torn off.

Again she tried to breathe into her husband's mouth, but her own breath was coming too hard for her to blow. Why did he feel so cold? Where were all the blankets she had packed?

"Thor! Get me a blanket!"

She heard the slow beep of the locator, its sound haunting and far away.

Someone would help Doug breathe when they found them.

"Hurry!" she prayed.

Just then, the feather tumbled slowly downward, touching Joe's lifeless outstretched hand as it fluttered out the door. Somehow she found a way to grab it and tuck it into her jeans. Only later would she notice that the red dot was gone.

Then Thor tugged again, this time managing to drag her a few feet. She felt herself slipping into darkness as he repeated the motion over and over, but the cold of the snow made her shiver, keeping her from blacking out.

The next thing she knew, she was lying under a tree about a hundred feet from the plane with Thor huddled beside her.

Then she saw the flames, and heard the explosion.

Suddenly, she felt warm again. Someone was telling her that she was in the hospital in Juneau and that Thor was being looked after by one of the staff.

"He saved your life," she heard a woman say.

Why was Sarah here?

"How . . .?"

She closed her eyes tightly, trying to squeeze out the scene, but someone was touching her now—gently on the shoulder, and reaching strong arms around to hold her even as she struggled to pull away.

"Wake up, Mara. We're home. Wake up. Everything is fine. We're all here. Hush for now, okay? You had a bad dream. Everything is fine," Doug was saying as he stroked her face.

When she opened her eyes and looked around, she was still sitting in the plane and Doug was right there, holding her in his arms, speaking soft words of comfort. Through the window, she could see their house in Hoonah and could see a worried-looking Sal and Joe waiting with Thor outside the plane.

When she looked at them, they waved anxiously. She blinked several times and looked around, trying to absorb what she saw. There was no hospital room, no Sarah, no wreckage, only the four of them near the house on a landing strip in Hoonah. She touched her face, her arms, and her legs. She touched Doug. Everything felt real.

"We're home now," Doug said, gently unbuckling her seatbelt. "We're all home now. It was only a bad dream."

Books By Marianne Schlegelmilch

One of America's Most gifted Writers

Feather From A Stranger
An Alaskan Mystery

Two Tickets and A Feather
Present Alaska—Future of her Past another Alaskan Mystery

Driftfeather on the Alaska Seas
Ultimate Future of the Past another Alaskan Mystery

Feather for Hoonah Joe
Alaska Can Be a Very Small Place

Raven's Light
A Tale of Alaska's White Raven

Gaston's Crow's Nest
An Alaska Tale

Solo Flite
An Alaska Puppy Becomes a Legend

Coho Waterboy
The Flat-Footed, web-Footed Alaska Sled Dog

Slugs Forever!
A Tale from an Alaska Backyard